"For the last time, Delahaye, stop asking questions. And get off me," Jenna ordered.

He smiled. The man smiled.

Her hand swung up along with her knee. Neither connected. With a grunt of pain he pulled her further underneath him. Despite the cavemanlike tactics, he'd been careful not to hit her injured ankle. That only made her angrier.

"You get your kicks bullying people?"

"No, that's your department!" he answered quickly.

Her mouth dropped open in shock. Then she remembered her ankle. "And don't coddle me, dammit," she sputtered. She wrestled beneath him, but rolling a redwood off her would have been easier.

"I love it when you get physical."

"Don't you dare condescend to me either."

"What, can't handle a little competition, Jenna? Am I getting in too close? Didn't you ever build defenses for that?" He leaned in closer. "Or didn't you think you'd need them?"

"You have no idea what I need."

"Oh, but I think I do. . . ."

WHAT ARE *LOVESWEPT* ROMANCES?

They are stories of true romance and touching emotion. We believe those two very important ingredients are constants in our highly sensual and very believable stories in the LOVESWEPT line. Our goal is to give you, the reader, stories of consistently high quality that may sometimes make you laugh, sometimes make you cry, but are always fresh and creative and contain many delightful surprises within their pages.

Most romance fans read an enormous number of books. Those they truly love, they keep. Others may be traded with friends and soon forgotten. We hope that each LOVESWEPT romance will be a treasure—a "keeper." We will always try to publish

LOVE STORIES YOU'LL NEVER FORGET BY AUTHORS YOU'LL ALWAYS REMEMBER

The Editors

Loveswept ® 857

LIGHT
MY FIRE

DONNA
KAUFFMAN

BANTAM BOOKS
NEW YORK · TORONTO · LONDON · SYDNEY · AUCKLAND

LIGHT MY FIRE
A Bantam Book / October 1997

ISBN 0-553-44577-4

Published simultaneously in the United States and Canada

Bantam Books are published by Bantam Books, a division of Bantam Dou-
bleday Dell Publishing Group, Inc. Its trademark, consisting of the words
"Bantam Books" and the portrayal of a rooster, is Registered in U.S.
Patent and Trademark Office and in other countries. Marca Registrada.
Bantam Books, 1540 Broadway, New York, New York 10036.

PRINTED IN THE UNITED STATES OF AMERICA
OPM   10 9 8 7 6 5 4 3 2 1

This book is dedicated to
Jean Hobday.

Not everyone is fortunate enough to
have a champion they can count on no
matter what. I have that and more.
You've been there for me from the
beginning and every day, good or bad,
since. I'm glad we could share this
one. I love you, Mom.

PROLOGUE

It was coming to get her.

She could feel the oppressive heat, hear the thundering roar. The ground vibrated. Life-snuffing smoke invaded the air, was sucked into her mouth, down her throat. She was gagging. She clawed at her neck. Choking. It was choking her.

Alive. How could anyone not see that? It moved, leaped, crawled. Lived, died. Killed. She'd learned to accept it was not her enemy. That acceptance had disappeared in the span of one lightning stroke.

She'd been a fool to think she had ever been in control. It would always be after her.

All she had to do was close her eyes.

Once again she was running through the forest, hot red-and-yellow flames licking at her boots, roaring in her ears. She heard the thunderous crack of another tree falling victim to the voracious predator. It rushed up the side of the mountain to meet them, consume them, growing as the wind lent a hand, encouraging the feeding frenzy. It crackled with a vicious snap, leaping easily over the fire line she and her crew had labored over for the past four hours, racing to gobble up more. Black smoke and tree soot sifted through the screen of her helmet, choking her. Her lungs burned. On she ran. Again she heard the bone-shaking crack as yet another tree lost the battle. She tensed, knowing what came next. What always came next.

The pain hit hard. Sharp and numbing. With a whooshing sound it rushed from its point of origin on her ankle to sweep over her entire body. She knew it was the tree, the burning tree. Her mind assembled all these things instantly, had her reaching for her fire cover even as it made first contact, even as she knew she was lost.

She heard Toby. Toby, her jump partner for four years, shouting at her, making her lift her head even as black shadows danced at the edges of her vision and heat began to crawl past the protective barrier of her flame-retardant suit. Pain and sound and smoke all swam together, making it hard to hear, impossible to focus. Then his face was in hers, shouting at her. She heard someone scream when the tree shifted. It was her. Screams ripped from her. Then a flash of silver billowed over her. Her fire cover. How had she gotten it out?

Toby's voice yanked her back from the edge. She felt the crushing weight of him and his gear, watched as he pulled the fire cover over him. Over them.

Light My Fire

3

The cover wouldn't hold, she knew that. It had been made to protect only one person. Toby knew that too. They hadn't cleared the ground of brush. She tried to yell past the knot of smoke in her throat, demand that he run, that he leave her, even as she knew they had both run out of time. Again she heard the rushing sound of the fire as it found them. As it ate them. The tree crushing her ankle succumbed first.

Toby succumbed second.

She heard him scream, felt him die as she waited in breathless terror for the first lick of searing heat, wondered in that split of eternal time what it would feel like. There was a nip, a taste. Heat; oh God the heat.

And then it was over.

In the capricious way of nature's disasters, the fire had roared on. And she had been left to survive. Survival of the damned.

Now it got even worse.

Shaking her head, as if simple denial would do any good, Jenna King thrashed, fear taking her breath in its terrifying clutches. She despised the fear. Almost as much as the heat. Oh, but it was hot. She'd never be cool enough again. She twisted, kicking, shoving at anything that covered her, oblivious to the spikes of pain shooting up her leg. The heat was worse than the pain could ever be.

A scream locked permanently in her throat. No. No! *You can't do this to me again!*

With a low, wrenching groan, Jenna grabbed at the anger, harnessed it, brandished it like a weapon, unleashing it full force on her enemy: fear. And the split second before she had to turn her head and look at what was left of Toby, she wrenched her eyes open and sat up.

Her room. She was in her room at Paradise Canyon. She blinked the sweat from her eyes, raked her hair back, and swung her gaze around, searching for reassurance, damning the semihysterical movement even as she fought to control it. Recognition of her surroundings came first. It always did. That base was what she needed most to center herself. Or so Dr. Porter had said. Breath came second. Once she drew in a lungful, she couldn't seem to stop. In no time she was gulping, panting. *Slow down, Jenna.* In. Out. The room is full of oxygen. There is plenty for you. No smoke here. No smoke.

The need to move came last. Thank God she could. She almost wept with relief, purposely shutting out the memories of those early months when she hadn't been able to. She shifted her legs over the side of the bed, barely flinching at the expected pain that went hand in hand with gravity.

She steadied herself before trying to stand. If she could focus on her recovery, she could put distance between herself and the recurrent nightmare. Then she could tuck it away, make herself believe she had dealt with it, that she controlled it, not the other way around. Eventually she might make herself believe she had won the battle with her mind.

She might succeed, if she could live without ever having to go to sleep again.

"Out of here," she mumbled. The words were hoarse. She would always sound rough, but she'd accepted that. It had been one of the easier things to get over. Still, first thing in the morning, all alone in her room, she always said something out loud before anyone else intruded into her day. It was sort of a gauge of how she was dealing with her life. Her new life.

She swore. This was one chapter of her new life she was closing. She needed to find control, to heal her mind.

"Well, things are about to change." She pulled off her damp sleep shirt and stood. Damning the shakes that rattled her body every morning, she moved gingerly, testing her ankle. It didn't feel too bad. It would never be perfect.

She struggled into cotton underwear and jeans, then yanked on a long waffle-knit undershirt and a heavy, oversized green henley. She stepped into the bathroom and looked into the mirror over the sink. "Today, Jenna King," she vowed, "today you take your life back."

She brushed her teeth, rebraided her hair, and swore heatedly as she struggled to get her hiking boots on. Then she very methodically gathered her clothes and the few other meager possessions she'd collected during her four-month stay at Paradise Canyon Rehabilitation Ranch, and shoved them into a pilfered canvas laundry bag.

And she worked very hard at not thinking about the fact that she had no life to take back.

ONE

T. J. Delahaye was all set to return to Paradise Canyon for his final seven A.M. therapy session when he found the bra.

He plucked it off the pine branch and untangled it. Guess this is what they mean by serviceable cotton, he thought, dangling the plain underwear from his fingers. He pulled several dried pine needles out of the cup. "38B." He uncurled the small white tag by the back hook and grinned. "Four weeks in the wilds of Oregon, but the man hasn't lost it."

Whistling, he tucked the bra in the back pocket of his jeans and did a little investigating. There was a break in the trees behind him, providing a panoramic peek of the rugged wilderness that was the Siskiyou Mountains. Nice enough place for a little interlude. Except there were no signs of a tussle—fun-loving or otherwise. He glanced past the pine tree, easily picking out the signs marking the path of a recent hiker. An apparently braless hiker.

Climbing these hills for the last several weeks, strengthening his newly healed body, hadn't been a cakewalk. Even whole and healthy, T.J. knew these trails would have given him more than a decent workout.

The woman wasn't sticking to the trail either. But then, T.J. understood the need to be a leader rather than a follower. He just hoped she hiked more efficiently than she packed.

He stilled, focusing his attention outward. His instincts, honed to a fine edge during a career made successful from listening to them, prickled along his consciousness. He looked back down the winding trail that led to Paradise. It was a twenty-minute hike. His appointment was in ten. His physiotherapist wasn't going to be real happy, but he didn't waste time worrying about that.

Dr. Dave shouldn't be too angry if he was a few minutes late, seeing as this was T.J.'s last session. That would give the good doctor, who was a young Arnold look-alike, a chance to hit on the new weight-room instructor. He decided to forge on.

Eleven minutes later he paused at the bend in the path, slightly winded. His explorations hadn't earned him any further insights into his quarry. Not so much as a pair of panties, cotton or otherwise, had marked the path. He should have turned back several minutes before. His knee was telling him in no uncertain terms that he'd pushed too far already.

You know things have gotten desperate, Delahaye, when you'll climb mountains to find a woman who wears white cotton underwear. He wished now he'd packed more than a canteen. A little food would go a long way at the moment. He'd only planned to be out to see one last sunrise, to meditate a little, soak in the surprising peace he'd discovered in the wild, unpredictable beauty of these mountains and canyons. He needed one last moment alone before returning to Denver, before accepting another assignment that would take him God knew where. If he had any more time to think, he was afraid he'd decide not to return at all.

But he was returning. That afternoon. He had his doctor's okay, and he had his plane ticket. It was just the lulling effect of his first break from the constant action in ten years that was making him think weird thoughts.

He cast another glance farther up the trail but shrugged and turned back. He'd endure one last lecture from Dave, get a good rubdown, then head out. He was scheduled for a debriefing with Scottie at the Dirty Dozen home base in Denver at three that afternoon. He was certain once he was back in the saddle, everything would fall into place. He'd feel like his normal, gung-ho self.

A sudden rushing noise followed by a high-pitched scream stopped him dead. He was running uphill, away from Paradise Canyon, his doctor, and his plane ticket, before he even made the conscious decision to do so. He focused on staying upright and not tripping, and ignored the rushing feeling of relief—and reprieve.

As soon as she came to a tumbling stop and realized she was still alive and mostly whole, Jenna let loose with every curse word she'd ever learned. Meticulous planning and attention to detail was her forte. In her profession it often meant the difference between life and death. *Yeah, but you don't belong to that profession anymore.*

It was the first time she'd let herself even think it. It hurt. Badly. It was also no excuse for her current predicament. But she was too busy feeling sorry for herself to let that minor detail slow her down.

Scowling, she groaned as she slid the strap of the laundry bag off her shoulder. Even with her crude modifications, it made a lousy backpack. She was certain it had left a permanent three-inch groove in her skin. She was also disgusted with herself. For a woman who'd routinely hiked with over seventy-five pounds of gear through rough terrain, it was hard to accept that the same sort of terrain had demolished her in under three hours, and she'd had fewer than twenty lousy pounds on her back.

"Pansy," she muttered, wanting to sound like the quick-thinking, self-disciplined Jenna King she used to be. Instead she sounded whiny.

She'd never tolerated whiners.

She didn't think she'd done any serious damage to herself—any new serious damage anyway—but she took the time to test out each joint and run a quick probe of her legs with her hands. There was pain. Steady, throbbing pain. For the last six months that pain had been her constant companion. As her heart rate returned to something close to normal, she conceded that there was more pain than usual.

Great. Just great. She didn't look up the incline behind her, not really interested at that moment in seeing how far she'd slid when the narrow path she'd been following around a large rock had suddenly crumbled under her feet.

She bent forward to carefully pick open the laces of her boot. Her hiking boots were the only item of clothing she'd forced her parents to bring to her. Not because she'd planned to go AWOL, but as a personal testament to her own will and drive. They had been a symbol to her, a goal.

She loosened the brown leather flap, giving in to a long, relieved groan as she slid the boot off. With increased blood flow, the pain intensified. She'd never get the thing back on. God, she thought, remembering her very vocal defiance six months before. In the face of insurmountable odds, she'd declared nothing would stop her from returning to her career as a forest firefighter and member of one of the elite smoke-jumping teams. How painfully pathetic she must have appeared to everyone, especially her parents.

Difficulties aside, and they had years of them under their belts, they loved her. That was one thing she didn't doubt. It was why she'd agreed to come to Paradise Canyon Rehab Ranch instead of heading back to Missoula to lick her considerable wounds in private.

She stared at her discarded boot. A symbol still, but now of defeat. What in the hell was she going to do?

"Hey, you okay down there?"

Jenna jumped, instinctively reaching for her pulaski or chain saw, feeling foolish and unreasonably angry when her fingers encountered nothing more than a laundry bag stuffed full of clothes.

She swore again, both at herself and at the fresh wave of hot pain lancing up her leg where she'd banged her ankle when she'd jumped. Wonderful. Out in the middle of nowhere, and she still managed to have an audience for her latest humiliation. Couldn't she catch one break?

"Hey! Can you hear me?"

"Yeah," she yelled halfheartedly. "I can hear you fine."

"Are you hurt?"

"Just my ego," she muttered. But she supposed that's what she got for thinking it was okay to have one. "I'm fine," she yelled. "Just peachy," she added under her breath.

"I don't have any gear. I'll have to go for help. It's gonna take an hour or so. Will you be okay until then? Or do you need immediate assistance?"

It was probably the acoustics of the canyon she'd half dropped into, but his voice was amazingly deep. It sort of rumbled down the slope and washed over her in a soft, soothing wave of sound that made her want to sigh and lie down to await rescue.

Jenna snorted and straightened. She must have hit her head on the way down. She'd always done the rescuing, not the other way around. She'd been on the other side the last time. Never again.

Of course, sticking by her decision was going to make getting off the side of the mountain a bit complicated.

She sighed, hating that she was once again forced to rely on someone else. She knew she should feel grateful. It was amazingly fortunate that another hiker had been close enough to hear her scream. But she really wanted to be alone. She'd started out that morning determined to make it on her own no matter what. One little detour down the mountainside wasn't going to change that.

No matter what her ankle was telling her.

"I'll be fine, really," she called up. She turned to look up at her volunteer savior, but the rising sun had found a temporary hole in the growing cloud cover and sliced through it in a blinding dagger of light. Shielding her eyes didn't do much more than show her a giant shadowy outline at the top of the embankment. She couldn't discern how much was man and how much was boulder. "Thanks anyway," she shouted.

There was a pause, then: "You sound a little rough. If you don't mind, I'll wait for you to catch your breath and make sure you can get back up here."

He really did have the most amazing voice. There was such steady strength and command in his tone.

"Can you climb?"

She scanned the rocky slope. Six months earlier she'd have attempted it. Even then it would have taken considerable skill and control. She scowled and sat up straighter. So she'd find another way off the mountain, preferably a less direct route. She'd been heading for the highway on the other side of the ridge, not wanting to catch a ride from anyone who might be coming to or going from Paradise. She'd left a note and an address in case there was any further paperwork for her to sign.

Despite it being against her doctor's recommendation, she was fully within her right to check herself out. The hike had become a personal challenge.

She'd taken short trails for the last month and during the last week she'd been making her own trails, progressively testing her ankle and the newly healed skin on her leg. The previous Friday, she'd hiked to the peak and back.

She wasn't ready to admit defeat yet. She looked downslope. She was sitting in a narrow depression on an otherwise smooth drop almost straight down. The hill bottomed out in a shallow but rocky ravine. If she tried to so much as stand, she'd likely take a shortcut straight into it. Even if her ankle would have allowed it, the steepness combined with the unstable footing made a controlled slide impossible. That left a parallel route. But a quick scan to her left and right wasn't too heartening. It was at least a hundred-yard crawl either way, and the indentation she sat on only spread out about twenty yards to each side of her.

Her options were quickly dwindling to one. A low, ominous rumbling cut into her thoughts. Cloud cover that was supposed to burn off as the sun rose had suddenly collected into a menacing-looking mass. She shivered, telling herself it was a reaction to the first gust of wind. It whipped up the fine rock dust, making her squeeze her eyes shut. Thunder rolled ominously overhead. She worked to tamp down the whispers of panic trying to edge into her mind.

Shielding her eyes against the wind and dust, she looked uphill. "You'd better go!" she yelled. "I'll be okay!" Wet, but okay. She could—would—handle this.

"I can't leave you out here," he called back, his rumbling voice underscored by another roll of thunder. The combination sent new shivers over her skin. Stop it, Jenna. She'd spent too many hours—thousands of them—out in the woods to be afraid of a little thunderstorm.

A jagged bolt of light shot across the sky.

No, she wasn't afraid of thunderstorms. It was the fire-igniting lightning that terrified her.

"This shouldn't last too long," she called out, her voice getting rougher from yelling but thankfully steady.

Big fat raindrops began to splatter the ground. She had no idea how experienced a hiker he might be, but if he wasn't carrying rope, then chances were he was an amateur. She ignored the point that she, a highly trained professional, had nothing more than a laundry-bag string on her supply list.

She tried not to look at the rocky ravine below. If the storm was strong enough and hit hard enough, with nothing but a laundry bag as an anchor, she could easily end up at the bottom anyway.

"Find shelter," she instructed, yelling louder over the growing noise as the storm gathered strength. "When it's over, bring some help back with you."

That should appease his sense of duty, get him off the mountain as safely as possible—and provide someone to help him scrape her stupid carcass off the side of this hill.

What was one more battering punch to her pride at this point anyway?

Wind whipped up again, enough so she could begin to feel the dampness right on through to her long underwear. Her Samaritan hadn't responded to her last shout. A quick, bleary peek uphill between wind gusts showed the dark outline had grown smaller. Considerably smaller.

He was gone.

Good. She rubbed her arms. He'd be okay. And so would she. He'd get help. If she was really lucky, it would be from somewhere other than Paradise Canyon, but she knew it was the only place of any size around for miles. Was he a patient there as well? she wondered.

Thunder shook the ground, loosening small surface rock, sending it skittering down and around her. She scraped the curly hairs escaping her braid from her forehead and eyes and pulled the long, thick plait over her shoulder so it hung between her breasts. She grabbed for the laundry bag, stuffing it between her thighs and as much of it under her shirt as she could, hoping to keep something dry enough to change into after the storm. She grabbed for her boot, and was debating whether her swollen ankle would tolerate her putting it back on or if she should tuck it into the laundry bag, too, when a sudden shout rang out.

She shifted around in time to see a black shadow tip off the edge of the embankment from the other side of the boulder, sending a fresh shower of rocks hailing down on her. She batted them away, a scream locked in her throat as the shadow materialized, through the sheets of rain, into a man. A very large man. A very large tumbling man.

And he was heading right toward her.

TWO

Don't hit her. Don't hit her.

T.J. tried to pull into a ball, knowing it would increase his speed, but hoping it would keep him from blasting her down the mountainside with him. Rocks, small and large, tore at his clothes. Gravel and sand pounded their way inside his sodden clothes and chewed at his skin. The world was a wild, wet kaleidoscope of color and pain.

Time was a furious whirl that stretched out one eerily long second at a time. He should have gone back for help instead of trying to find a path down to her. She'd certainly sounded tough enough. He pulled his head into a tighter tucked position, ignoring the bites the mountainside was taking out of his hide, instead seeing in his mind's eye how she'd flinched when the lightning had zigzagged across the sky. He couldn't leave her there.

Was he past her by now? Surely he had to be.

She'd be okay. She had to be. He didn't think about what awaited him at the bottom. He'd do it again if given a choice.

The last thing that went through his mind before he met an abrupt, unconscious end was that he was going to miss his plane now for sure.

Jenna's quick lateral scramble had removed her from the direct path of the man's unexpected descent. There had been a panicked, slippery second or two when she thought she would follow him, but she'd kept her tenuous perch. However, his size and speed had loosened much of the rocks and gravel in his path, all of which was tumbling down in a bouncing rush, despite the now heavy rain.

She ducked her head as smaller rocks started pinging down on her back and shoulders. She didn't dare look to see if anything larger was heading her way.

She also didn't dare look at the ravine below her.

She wasn't too proud of herself at the moment. These last several hours had forced her to acknowledge several painful truths, and apparently her lessons weren't over yet. That thought made her angry—at herself for allowing fear to gain another hold on her and at the continued onslaught of circumstances that always seemed beyond her control. Hadn't she faced enough?

She was still grappling with the harsh reality that her body was really and truly going to betray her and never heal one hundred percent. Her body—its strength, power, and size—had been the one constant and reliable factor in her life, the one thing over which she had had ultimate control.

She'd also always understood that along with a strong body, one needed a strong mind. She'd prided herself on having both. Now one was gone, or at least useless to her in the life she'd built for herself. But the other . . .

Jenna started to tremble. Teeth clenched against the pain shooting from her ankle, she carefully pulled her knees in tighter and clamped her arms around them, burrowing her head as deeply as possible. Her trembling escalated to shaking.

Dear God, she whispered silently. Please don't do this to me. Stranded on a mountainside in a downpour in the middle of God knew where, she'd come up against the final wall. And this time her mind wasn't going to be strong enough to haul her up over it.

Nightmare images flashed through her head. Toby. Oh, Toby. Then his face shifted to one younger, one so innocent. Jonny. Her eyes burned, and it was only then that she realized they were squeezed shut.

You have to look, Jenna. You have to look and see if he's okay.

Okay? Of course he wasn't okay! She felt an overwhelming urge to laugh hysterically. No one could fault her for losing it. And that's exactly what terrified her the most. No matter how strong she tried to be, she wasn't going to be able to hold it together. Her mind would betray her too. And once it was lost, she'd never get it back.

A low rumble reached her ears. Thunder. Maybe lightning would finish off what it had started and strike her dead. The rumble reached her ears again. Even with her head down and eyes squeezed shut, she knew there had been no lightning strikes. Which meant . . .

No. He was at least thirty yards below her. She couldn't hear him. As if to prove her wrong, the rumble returned, then edged into a long, agonized groan.

Somehow she stilled further. Perhaps her heartbeat had stopped too. He was alive.

For now.

Look, Jenna. Find a way to get down there and help.

Terror paralyzed her every muscle, her every nerve. No. No no no no no no. I can't. *You have to. He needs help.*

She wanted to shut out the rest, but her own mind betrayed her. *He's down there because he tried to help you.*

Like Toby. Like Jonny.

And, like them, he'd die for his trouble.

The brutal truth sliced into her like a hot knife, its blade dull enough to rend jagged tears in her psyche. She shook uncontrollably. *Yes!* she wanted to scream. Dead. All dead. I couldn't save Toby or Jonny. I can't save this stranger. Sobs began to choke her. *I can't even save me.*

"Help . . . me." The guttural words crawled up

the side of the ravine and burrowed into what was left of her mind.

A sudden fury took hold of her. Like a wildfire ignited by a single bolt of lightning, the rage grew fast and swift, overwhelming the fear, the hate, the guilt, the pain. She threw back her head, opened her hot, dry eyes to the sky, and shouted at the top of her lungs. *"No! I can't do this anymore!"*

Rain blinded her. Then the ground shifted out from under her. A second later she was sliding downward, fast and out of control. Sliding toward the rock-strewn ravine. Sliding toward the man who'd tried to save her when he should have saved himself.

Sliding uncontrollably toward her fate.

She closed her eyes and gave in to the fall, wondering why she'd ever fought it in the first place.

T.J. carefully lifted his head, then wished he hadn't. He had no idea how badly he was hurt, or exactly what parts of him were damaged.

He'd been out, but for how long, he had no idea. Loud groaning, his own probably, had stirred him awake. He was happy to be alive, though perhaps relieved was a better word. Nothing about him was happy at the moment. Move, he had to move. He shifted his chin. Yep, he was alive all right, but he'd rather not be awake.

But there was some reason why. . . . His mouth suddenly filled with sandy gritty water. Oh yeah. The ravine was filling up with water. He either had to move or drown.

Move it out, Delahaye. He hadn't survived the fall—survive being a relative term at the moment—to drown in a puddle. But the puddle was rapidly becoming a stream. And he knew enough about these canyons to know that a stream could easily become a raging river during a flash storm.

With no time to assess damage or the potential for aggravating it by moving the wrong way, T.J. managed to shift the arms trapped under him so that his palms were pressed down. Sharp rocks pierced his already abraded skin as he pressed up, but his legs failed him at the last moment, sending him onto his side with a loud grunt of pain.

At least with this side of his face up, the rain washed the grit away. He blinked his eyes open. Then blinked again. There was something . . . a dark shape. . . .

He couldn't lift his hand to wipe his face, and shaking the water off was a no go if he wanted to stay conscious.

Then he realized that the dark shape was growing in size, and that it was headed right at him.

Apparently he hadn't missed her after all.

He had little time to brace himself for the impact. He rolled forward and lifted his arm. At least he could break her fall, he thought. A second later his world exploded in a fresh rainbow of pain as she barreled into him.

T.J. fought against the black void that threatened

again and opened his eyes despite his fierce desire to do otherwise. He was partly on his side, partly on his back. Judging by the pressure bearing him deeper into the jagged surface, his distressed damsel was sprawled on top of him.

Something that felt like wet hair was clinging to his head and neck, half covering his face. He inched his hand up to peel it off. She lifted her head as his hand encountered sodden fabric.

He blinked away the rain and found deep brown eyes staring into his.

"You've got my underwear on your head."

Trapped on a mountainside, injured, about to drown in a flash flood, T.J. smiled. So serious, his damsel. He raked the white cotton panties off his face. "If I knew you were going to drop in," he said with a grimace of pain, "I would have picked up first."

"You're hurt."

She hadn't returned his smile, which faded at her accusatory tone. "Funny how that happens when you take a header down a mountain. No gold medal for me today."

Her so-serious eyes narrowed, wet eyelashes jutting out in spikes like angry exclamation points. "You think almost dying is funny?"

He had no idea why she was angry with him. Shock perhaps. "I've almost died lots of times," he said, the expression on his face smooth and open. He knew he took some getting used to, but her reaction was unique. "You have to develop a sense of humor about it after a while, otherwise you'll go nuts."

Her look made it clear she thought he'd reached that pinnacle already.

"Are you okay? Two falls in one day—"

"Peachy." He hadn't missed the shadow that had crossed her rain-drenched features. She sounded rough. Very rough. And not remotely peachy. How much pain was she trying to hide? Her face was pale, but the chill of the rain made it difficult to determine normal skin tone. Long strands of hair clung to her face and neck, the rest was pulled back into a braid that was long enough to be trapped between them. Blond, he guessed. Maybe a light brown. There were no obvious cuts or abrasions on her head or neck, which was all of her he could see in his current position.

Her face was broad, her hairstyle emphasizing the smooth, even features of her no-nonsense nose and firm mouth and chin. No sharp edges, he thought, then swallowed a smile. Unless he counted the ones in her eyes and on the sides of her tongue. Not your standard beauty, rain-soaked or otherwise, T.J. decided, but compelling. Most definitely compelling.

He shivered as water rushed over his legs and between their bodies. "We have to get out of this ditch before we drown."

"Yeah, that would ruin the day, wouldn't it."

A lot had happened to her in a short period of time, yet there was no panic in her expression or tone. His experience with hostage removal had taught him people usually fell into two categories: those who focused on how to end their incarceration and those who focused on how they got incarcerated in the first place. He was betting she was the former.

"Problem is," he went on, "I'm not sure I can move without some help. Are you injured? Can you move?"

She hadn't moved more than her mouth since she'd landed on him. "My ankle's out," she stated unemotionally. "Everything else is minor."

He was impressed with her control, but that didn't diminish his concern. She seemed almost detached from what was happening. Perhaps she'd had some sort of prior climbing experience.

Before he could suggest a plan, she was looking around, assessing the situation. "It'll be easier on both of us if I go over you and up the other side," she said, her eyes scanning the incline of the opposite side of the ravine. It wasn't too steep and leveled off about twenty yards up. If they could get to the top, they'd be out of the direct danger of the raging river the ravine was swiftly becoming.

"Can you take more of my weight?" she asked. Blinking the rain from her eyes, she ran a quick gaze over him.

He could feel her weight stretched out over most of him. He was six-seven, which meant she wasn't a small woman. He found himself bemused by that idea.

"You ready?" Her eyes were on his again, steady, but otherwise impossible to read.

"You need me to lift you?" He tried to work his

other hand free, but it forced his weight back too much. He winced and swore under his breath.

"Don't move," she ordered. "I'm going to reach across you and use that large rock above your shoulder for leverage. It's wedged in deep and shouldn't move. Once I have a good grip, I'll use my good leg to push myself off of you."

"Do it," he said, then braced himself.

To her continued credit, she didn't question him. A few excruciating seconds later she was off of him and seated at an awkward angle on the sharp incline of the ravine. If the move had caused her pain, she hadn't let it show by so much as a grimace. But it was clear she was favoring her right leg.

The rain wasn't abating at all, and neither was the rising water. It now rushed over his waist. Slowly, carefully, T.J. pushed himself up on one arm, rapidly assessing his condition as he did.

"My left knee is shot," he said between gasps of air. His right shoulder wasn't too happy with him either. He looked up to her, his smile more grimace than grin. "Some rescue attempt, huh?"

He was surprised and disappointed to see the banked fury return to her eyes. He'd expected relief, concern, even fear. He didn't know what to make of her. Now was not the time to wonder, though. The water was rising fast. He could feel the pull of it on his legs.

"Can you get higher up the side? I need some leverage to pull myself out of here."

Without comment, she efficiently did as he asked.

He noted she did her best not to send more rocks skittering down on him. He turned away from her and concentrated on hoisting himself out of there. The angle at which he'd landed made using his good arm impossible. Typical. He clenched his teeth, reached up for a good hold on the same jutting rock she'd—

"What's your name?" he asked abruptly, suddenly needing to know.

Her brows raised in surprise, but she said, "Jenna."

He tested the rock against his strength, then with a mighty groan and a healthy string of swear words that he tried to keep under his breath, he pulled himself up, dragging his lower body out of the raging flow of water. He rolled to his stomach and grabbed another rock and pulled again. His shoulder screamed, but he didn't stop until his feet were above flood level. He rolled carefully onto his back, thankful finally to be on relatively smooth surface. He let the rain pound him for a moment, then turned his head slightly and opened his eyes.

She was sitting several feet away, one hand rubbing her outstretched leg. She'd been staring at him and made no attempt now to pretend otherwise.

He reached out his hand. "T. J. Delahaye. Interesting to meet you."

No smile. No handshake.

He let his hand drop along with any further attempt at friendly chatter. "This doesn't look like it's going to let up. We need to find some shelter." He angled a glance to the sky. "At least the thunder and lightning stopped."

He shifted his gaze in time to catch her slight involuntary shudder. His fearless damsel, afraid of thunderstorms? That could explain her behavior. Some people vented fear as anger, especially when the source of their fear was inescapable.

He could have shared his feelings on thunder and lightning, but he doubted she'd appreciate his insights into storms or into her. "How well do you know this area?" he asked instead.

"Up there?" She nodded toward the trail they'd both descended from. "Pretty well. Down here? Not very."

At least she was answering him. "Not from around here?"

"Are you?" she asked by way of response.

"No. I had family up in the north part of the state, Clackamas County area, but they're all gone now. This is my first time back in Oregon in almost twenty years." He'd been surprised by the strong sense of homecoming he'd felt, but he didn't share that with her.

She made no comment and didn't offer up any information about herself. T.J. stifled a sigh, not sure why he was even trying. He needed to get them somewhere safe and out of the elements, a place where he could more thoroughly assess the situation. They didn't have to be pals to work together as partners in their own rescue, but a little friendly cooperation wouldn't have hurt.

"I've hiked out here for the last several weeks, but until now I've managed to stay on the top part of the mountain." He smiled despite her scowl. "I don't know this area well at all. But there has to be shelter somewhere. The problem is getting us to it."

She nodded to the water, which had already risen to his feet. "I think we need to get out of this ravine first."

T.J. eyed the area he'd vacated, which was now under water. It had been an unusually dry summer followed by an even drier and warmer fall. There had been much discussion at Paradise about the horrendous forest fires of the past season, which had claimed hundreds of thousands of acres in Jackson and Klamath counties, all the way into northern California.

The fires were out now, but the dry ground couldn't absorb heavy downpours swiftly enough, which meant flash flooding. As the front moved farther in, the storm would eventually abate to a steady rain that would feed the earth instead of pummel it. Even with the cooler air the storm had brought, the unusually warm late-October weather made it tolerable for them. He was only chilled to the bone instead of frozen solid.

"Can you pull yourself up to the top?" he asked. "It might take me a bit longer, but I can manage." For the first time he noticed the heavy string diagonally crossing her chest. He looked across the ravine at the steep incline they'd both tumbled down. There were spots of white, gray, and dark blue clinging in unrecognizable lumps to some of the larger rocks. Her clothes.

He thought of the bra he'd found on the tree what now seemed like days ago. "What kind of backpack are you carrying anyway?"

She followed his gaze, and he watched as she noted her belongings strewn across the mountainside, far out of reach now with a wall of water between them. If the loss bothered her, she didn't let on. Her expression was flat when she turned back to him. She didn't acknowledge the sack slung on her back in any way, but merely said, "Not a very good one, apparently."

She was a tough one. And there was definitely something more motivating her oddly detached anger than fear. Given his size, he'd worry that she was concerned about her safety. In his current condition, however, that wasn't really an issue. And she hadn't seemed the least bit afraid of him when she was sprawled all over him, nor had she exhibited any sort of relief when she'd crawled away. She was a capable, controlled person, clearly not intimidated by her predicament or by him.

He also couldn't ignore the fact that she'd been out hiking off trail on a rugged mountainside with her clothes her only possessions.

What was wrong with this picture? What was wrong with him for spending time he didn't have wondering about it?

T.J. shoved the puzzle aside. Getting them out of there was—had to be—his focus. His only focus.

THREE

Jenna scrabbled around for another secure handhold, trying not to send too many more rocks tumbling down on T.J.'s head. Not that caring for him was her responsibility. He'd chosen to stay on the trail, to try that foolhardy rescue attempt. She'd told him to go find shelter, go find help. Qualified help. Now they were both stuck. And she didn't like it, not one tiny bit.

Tiny. Now there was a word that no one would use to describe anything about her erstwhile rescuer, she thought, grimacing as the next handhold dug into her already scraped palm. The man was a giant. At six-foot-two herself, she felt she was in a perfect position to judge.

She put all she had into her upper body, dragging her leg as carefully as she could. Reaching for another rock hold, she winced as a sharp edge caught a raw area, but focused on the pain rather than remembering how it felt to be stretched out all over his huge hard body and discovering there was still man to spare.

She peered up and let out a long sigh. Only another yard or two, and she'd be at the top. She glanced down past her shoulder to see if Delahaye was following her. He'd only managed to move out of the water by about three or four feet. Jenna hardened herself to the tight ball centered in her chest. She was having a hard enough time taking care of herself. She couldn't worry about him.

But she couldn't ignore the mental picture she had of him right after he'd pulled himself from the water. Despite wide, even features, thick lashes surrounding warm blue eyes, and a mouth that seemed permanently curved upward in a teasing smile, he hadn't looked so good. His skin had been pale and he'd been banged up pretty good.

Not your problem, Jenna. Still, she waited until he'd grabbed another rock and pulled before looking away.

"You almost there?" he called out.

His voice was considerably rougher, even deeper than hers, she thought dryly. "Another foot," she shouted.

With one last good pull, she dragged herself up onto flat ground. She took a moment to catch her breath, then scooted sideways and turned to see what progress he was making. He'd gotten another yard maybe. Not good.

Muttering to herself, she rolled to a sitting position and gently massaged her leg. Her wet jeans felt like sandpaper on her grafted skin. She pulled her hand away, scraped the straggles of wet hair from her face and neck, and scanned the area.

There was another ridge just north of where she sat, but the dense forestation made it hard to tell how far up it was or what terrain fell in between.

A sharp grunt followed by a scraping sound brought her head back around. She looked down and swore. The rock he'd grabbed for support had popped loose, sending him sliding back down, losing about half the distance he'd gained. She eyed the still-rising water. By her estimate it had been less than fifteen minutes since he'd tumbled to the bottom of the ravine and no more than a half hour since it had started raining. The water was deepening rapidly, meaning one or more nearby feeder streams was flooding, adding to the flow at a considerably faster pace.

She had to get him out of there. Dammit, she hadn't asked for his interference. She watched him reach for a fresh handhold. The man was no quitter.

And neither are you.

"Yeah, yeah, yeah," she grumbled, already scooting across the ground and reaching for the longest branch she could find. *And look where that got me*, she added silently.

"Here!" She had to shout to be heard over both the rain and the rushing water. He looked up, and she shoved the branch over the edge, angling the end toward him. It would provide an easy handhold. She scooted as far back from the edge as she could and still keep the branch level with the decline, then began digging in hard with her good foot. Thank heavens she'd only taken off one boot.

The first tug took her right to the edge. "Hold up!" He was going to take her right back down there with him. They'd both drown. She hadn't come this far to die. And she'd be damned if she'd let Delahaye add himself to her list of guilty sins. Her burden was quite heavy enough already, thank you.

He'd let go of the branch and was trying to use the rocks again, but the continued rain had loosened even the bigger ones. "Hold on," she called, and pointed to the heavy branch. "Hold on, but don't move for a minute." She wasn't sure he heard all of it, but he grabbed the wood and didn't tug. She wasted no time in ripping the laundry bag over her head. Thank God for nylon cord. The rain made it a bit slick, but she picked at the knot and managed to get it undone. She dared a peek over the edge.

The water was halfway up his knees.

She moved faster, looping one end quickly around the few broken limbs of the branch she had at her end, then scooting back to tie it around the tree. It wasn't quite long enough! She tore into the bag, finally dumping what was left on the ground. She rooted around in the meager remains but couldn't find what she needed. Damn.

She looked at the tree and had another idea. She hated it, but there was no time for anything else. She grabbed a sodden sweatshirt, slid around behind the slender but sturdy trunk and straddled it, then reached around on either side and grabbed the loop end of the rope. She just made it.

Man, this was not going to be fun. She wedged the sweatshirt between her face and the trunk, then yelled, "Climb!"

She felt a tentative tug. No way was that moving him. "I'm anchored to a tree," she shouted. "Climb, climb!"

An instant later she was one with the tree. Her shoulder muscles screamed, the back of her wrists rubbed raw where she'd wrapped the cord over them. She dug in with her good foot to try to alleviate the strain and keep the bark from penetrating the shirt and permanently embedding itself into her body.

Do it, do it, do it.

Her back started to cramp. Just when she thought she couldn't last another second, the pressure suddenly stopped, flinging her backward with the release. A loud groan escaped her clenched teeth when her backward motion pulled the branch tight up to the tree, yanking once again on her wrists.

Her first thought was he'd let go and fallen, but then she heard a heavy groan, followed by the dull thud and ground vibration of his body collapsing nearby.

"You okay?" His gravelly voice barely reached her.

Peachy, she thought, slowly uncurling her hands from their cramped grip on the nylon cord. The scrapes from her earlier tumbles had rubbed open, and she turned them palm up to allow the rain to cleanse them. She whistled in a breath on the slight sting, then slowly curled and extended her fingers.

"My hands are a little cramped is all. I'm fine."

She heard him grunt and looked around the tree. He was less than a yard away, on his stomach. She saw him try to push himself upright.

"Don't move," she said. "Lie there and rest. It's no big deal."

He grunted as he pushed once again, then slumped back to the ground, though she imagined it was more from necessity than from obedience to her command.

"You're an amazing woman, Jenna," he said, the words muffled against the wet ground. "Ornery as hell, but amazing."

"Yeah, well, that and a quarter will get me a cup of coffee."

He lifted his head. *"That* saved my life." His hair was plastered over his forehead and eyebrows, but his sharp gaze pierced through the clinging tendrils.

She should ignore him and concentrate on her own problems, like getting the hell out of there. But she heard herself say, "Which thing would that be? My being ornery or amazing?"

He stared at her for a second, then his mouth kicked up, pushing dimples into the pale, wet skin on either side. "Both."

The man was a lunatic. Only a lunatic would smile at such a time. It was an uncomfortable conclusion to reach, since she felt the tug on the corners of her own mouth.

She looked down at her hands. Since when did she care what others thought of her? Most especially men?

Jenna King, Amazon Queen. How many times had she heard those words? Over the years the jeer had taken on more adult overtones, from fellow workers and friends alike. Once an Amazon, always an Amazon. Jenna didn't fool herself on that score. She'd always felt like an outcast.

She ignored her realization that respect, admiration, and even awe hadn't made her feel any more a real part of the group. She wasn't normal. She'd always been on the fringe. And that was how she liked it. At least as a figure of respect they let her have her peace. Deep into her thoughts, she never heard him move.

"What the hell did you do to your hands?"

She jumped, wincing at the flare of pain in her ankle, then glared at him. "I chewed them up a little playing human pulley."

He was sprawled on his side next to her, wedged up on one elbow. For the first time she got a really good idea of just how big he was. And he thought *she* was amazing. The man was a monstrosity of muscle wrapped in ragged flannel and denim. Even bone-dry and buck naked he'd blow out a normal set of scales. He was easily half a foot over six feet, with shoulders an ox would envy and legs almost as big as the tree trunk her own were presently wrapped around. That brought an instant mental image that had her snapping her gaze back to his.

His eyes were a bright, little-boy blue, and his damn dimples were winking at her again. "I eat all my vegetables."

She imagined an entire salad bar would be a light snack for this man. She was stranded with Paul Bunyan.

He nudged himself forward until his head was near her knee. He nodded to her hands. "Let me see?" He was propped on his left arm, but he slid that hand over, palm up and open.

She looked at his right arm, which lay curled against his side. "Your shoulder?"

"Old injury revisited," he said dismissively. "Let me look at your hands." His eyes widened, then narrowed on hers. "They're bleeding."

"They're just scraped up."

"What in the hell did you do?" he asked once again. The guilt and remorse she saw in his eyes were familiar to her. It didn't soften her toward him in the least.

"I saved your soaking wet butt the only way I knew how."

"Why didn't you tie the cord to the branch?"

"Gee, why didn't I think of that?" He was lucky she didn't smack him with it. "It was a few inches short. I didn't have anything useful left to extend it with other than my arms."

He looked at the scattered remnants of clothes, then reached behind him and tugged something from his pocket. He let it drop in front of him. "I guess I should have given this back earlier. Would have come in handy."

Her bra. The man had been carrying her bra around in his back pocket? "It's not your size anyway."

"I found it on the trail. Or should I say off the trail. You know, you shouldn't—"

"You're alive, don't lecture me, okay? If you'd gone for help when I'd asked you to—oh, forget it. No use in crying over it now." She snatched up her bra and tossed it toward the bag.

"I'm sorry, Jenna." He waited. The pull of silence worked, and she finally looked at him. "I'm sorry about not going for help. I'm sorry you hurt yourself that way to save me. Thank you isn't enough."

Distinctly uncomfortable, she turned her attention to untangling her body from the tree. "Don't thank me. I didn't have to save your life. I wasn't responsible for the mess you got yourself in. I happened to be the only one here at the time."

"I couldn't leave you on the side of the hill, especially with the lightning—"

She turned on him. "I'm fully capable of taking care of myself."

"I can see that." She wanted to smack the smile off his face. "Now, at any rate," he added. "But then you were a huddled vulnerable-looking lump, and I couldn't walk away and leave you there."

She smoothed the scowl from her features. Damn the man for getting to her. But a "vulnerable-looking lump"? Oh how her crew would howl over that one. It shouldn't hurt, but it did.

"We both made mistakes," she stated evenly. "I'd say we're both paying for them. Let's worry about what to do next, okay?"

"We're not going to do anything much until this rain stops." He motioned toward the denser stand of pines about ten yards away. "I don't think either one of us is going to die from our injuries, but we could both use some rest and some time to figure out what our next move should be. If we can get ourselves over to those trees, that would provide some shelter and get us away from the ravine."

She didn't bother to point out that if the water rose far enough to swell over the ravine, they'd have to be a hell of lot farther away than ten yards to do any good.

"Let's do it." She scooted back from the tree. The effects of playing human pulley sang up her back and thighs, and she let slip one or two expletives.

"Ornery but colorful," he said.

"Shut up." She grabbed two relatively clean socks, wrapping one around each hand to pad her palms. She thought about scraping together what was left of her clothes, but shrugged the idea aside. She'd do that after the rain stopped. "You're on your own getting to the trees." She scooted backward, keeping her attention focused over her shoulder.

No vulnerable lump, she. T.J. smiled, recalling her reaction to that description. He definitely stood corrected. Or would if standing was an option at the moment.

"You gonna lie there all day in the rain, Delahaye?"

T.J. chuckled and tested his shoulder. He'd wrenched it pretty good, but it was nothing a little rest wouldn't take care of. His knee was a different story. One advantage to his size was his heavy bone mass. He was a hard man to break, but he was also a fast healer. In his line of work, that quality came in handy. Of course, the numerous members of the medical community who had worked on him over the last month and a half would not be happy that he'd taken a header down a mountain.

He turned toward Jenna, who was now leaning back against the biggest tree trunk in the stand. "Missing me already?" He focused on her responding scowl as he ungracefully crawled to her side. Once under the trees, he rolled to his back and attempted to relax each muscle.

After several moments she said, "You okay?"

"I've been better. About like you, I imagine." He lifted his head. Her wet, dirty-sock-clad foot was directly in his line of vision. "Isn't your foot cold?"

"I'm sure if I let myself think about it it will be."

Ornery. "What the hell happened to your boot?"

"I took it off. My ankle was swollen. I intended to put it back on but—"

"We played leapfrog instead." He tried to check out her ankle, but from his angle, he couldn't see it. "I don't suppose you put it in your bag, did you?"

She glared at him. "I don't suppose I did."

For some reason, her frown made him want to smile. He refused to give up on her. "Do you live out here somewhere?"

"Do you?"

He did smile this time, swallowing a groan as he shifted himself into an upright position. He leaned back against the tree and looked at her. Long strands of wet brown hair had been pulled from her braid and were wrapped across her neck and shoulders. A quick glance at her ankle proved the morning's activities had taken a further toll. Given that his knee felt like someone was driving a hot poker through it, he knew she had to be feeling the same thing. Yet to look into her large brown doe eyes, he'd never know it. She was so serious—and so evasive.

Even wet, wounded, and wasted, his radar was fully functional. He considered it a blessing. It gave him something else to think about besides his own pain.

"You should probably elevate that ankle." He shifted again so his thigh was near her foot.

"Don't."

He sighed. "It won't hurt me," he said, purposely misunderstanding her. "It's my other leg that's messed up." He met her hard gaze. "Listen, I know we haven't made a good team so far, but don't let that stop you from doing what's best for you."

"What would be best for me is you leaving me alone."

He didn't so much as blink. "Either you move your ankle, or I will."

Her gaze was unwavering, her foot unmoving.

He reached for her.

"Okay, okay. Don't touch me."

She carefully lifted her foot, then rested her calf on his thigh. The only signs that the movement had cost her were the tighter frown lines bracketing her mouth.

He looked back to her ankle. Her jeans covered the upper part, but he could still see that it had ballooned to easily twice its normal size. Even if she had her boot, she'd never get it on. "Did you twist it when you fell from the path?"

"Do you always ask so many questions?"

"Do you ever answer one?"

Now she sighed. "I hurt my ankle a while back. I pushed it a bit too hard today, and it gave out on me while I was circling that boulder. Happy?"

"Happy? No. Dry clothes, a nice hot breakfast, a ride to the airport, that would make me happy."

"Airport? You have a flight scheduled for today?"

"Had." Funny, he thought. It wasn't until he'd mentioned it that he realized he really wasn't sorry he'd missed it. He didn't want Scottie and the rest of the Dirty Dozen team to worry, but other than that, he didn't seem to care a whole lot.

"Well, if you had someplace to go, why in the hell didn't you go back and send help when I asked you? You could have made your flight, and I'd be off this mountain by now. Don't you have any common sense?"

"I've always thought I had a fair share. Until I ran into you."

She rolled her eyes. "Very bad pun."

"I hadn't intended to do more than watch one last sunrise this morning. I was on my way back, in fact, when I found your bra." He smiled at her scowl. He was beginning to like it. At least it was a more interesting reaction than anger. Or fear. "Anyway, maybe I wasn't in as much of a hurry to get back as I thought." He didn't mention his internal radar. He doubted she'd be impressed. "I decided to follow your trail. But you didn't leave any more lingerie crumbs, and it was getting late, so I'd decided to turn back. That's when I heard you scream." He shifted against the trunk and the ache in his shoulder began to ease. "Believe it or not, I'm trained to know better. But I couldn't leave you on the side of the mountain to face this storm alone."

Emotion flashed through her eyes, but before he could tag it, it was gone. "You're trained? No backpack, no supplies, no rope? What are you trained to do?"

T.J. shifted to face her. "I rescue people." It was worth the dagger of pain. She laughed.

FOUR

Jenna's laughter died quickly. "You really do think you're Paul Bunyan." It was obviously not the first time someone had made the comparison. She, of all people, should have been more sensitive to that. "I'm sorry, that was uncalled for."

"Not a problem. There's worse things than being compared to a legendary hero."

Jenna didn't know what else to say. He was staring up at the trees. The rain had almost stopped, only a scattering of droplets made it through the high branches. He wasn't angry, but he wasn't smiling either. Something was wrong. Until now the man's face had been grooved in a permanent grin.

She told herself to be thankful for the quiet, to be thankful that he'd stopped questioning her. She didn't want to talk about herself. She had an even harder time admitting to need. She'd had months of it, and right now she wanted only to need herself. But despite his annoying good-spiritedness, she didn't want him to shut her out.

"You said you hadn't been back to Oregon in twenty years. That's a long time." She waited a beat, but he didn't look surprised at her first foray into polite conversation. In fact, he didn't look at her at all. "What brought you back?"

He didn't answer. She'd begun to think he was paying her back for her own refusal to talk, when he said, "I got injured and I had to pick a place to rehab when I got out of the hospital." He paused a moment, long enough for her to admit to herself that she really wanted to know the rest.

"I work out of Colorado," he said. "Oregon was on the list of available rehab locations, so I figured, why not?"

"You were at Paradise Canyon?"

He looked over at her. "Yes. You know the place?"

She grimaced. "Inside and out."

"Ah, another happy Canyon camper. What were you in for? The ankle?"

She looked down at the ground. How had they ended up talking about her again? "I don't remember seeing you."

"My 'incarceration' was brief, only a few weeks. It's a big place. I guess we were on different schedules."

"Apparently." Steering the subject firmly back to him, she said, "So, you heading back to Colorado to rescue more people?"

"As soon as I complete this mission." He grinned.

It made his eyes twinkle. He really looked the quint-essential gentle giant. But she hadn't forgotten the steel in his black velvet voice when he'd bullied her into propping up her foot on his thigh. Her ankle did feel better. At least the pain had settled into a low, steady throb. She found her gaze wandering to his legs. His thigh was tree-trunk huge and just as hard. The rain had molded the denim to his legs, outlining wide, strong-looking calves. Her soggy sock-clad ankle looked almost delicate in comparison.

The very idea made her smile.

"Hey, don't count me out yet," he said, misunder-standing. "I may look down—" She arched her brow. His grin widened. "Okay, so I am down, but I'm very resourceful."

"Thanks, but I think I'll take my chances and rely on myself." He didn't say anything, but his smile faded as he continued to study her. Hers faded too, but she didn't look away.

"I don't think I've ever met anyone quite like you."

"We're even, then." Here it comes, she thought. The inevitable my-you're-so-strong-you're-so-big-you're-so . . . so Amazon. She'd lost track of how many times she'd suffered through these "Jenna the Giant" conversations. It had been a long while since she'd let them get to her. She was surprised at how disappointed she felt. Maybe because he was larger than life, too, she thought he'd be different.

"Look at it this way," she said, her tone more

defensive than she'd intended. "At least I won't ever ask you to get something off the top shelf for me."

His laugh surprised her. "I wasn't talking about your height, short stuff. I can't say for sure since we've spent most of our limited acquaintance lying down, but judging from our earlier position in the ravine, I'd say I've got a good half foot on you."

Jenna swallowed hard. She remembered exactly what he'd felt like beneath her—hard, powerful, and big. She flashed to the thought of what it would be like to lie beneath him, to feel his body pin hers down, to feel his strong arms move around her, to nuzzle her face in that too-broad-to-be-real chest.

Heat from a long-ignored source flickered to life deep inside her. It felt too good, and she was too cold and wet and miserable to snuff it out.

It wasn't until she reached his smiling face and twinkling eyes that she realized she'd been visually cataloging his entire body—and with a look that no doubt said she was ready to place her order.

This time the rush of heat centered in her cheeks. Every man who had ever caught her attention had always come up short—literally. Sometimes she tried to ignore it, but most times it was impossible to get past the mental stumbling block.

It occurred to her that this time, for the first time, that wasn't the case.

Rallying back, she said, "Short stuff?"

"Hey, don't take it too hard. You can't always be queen of the mountain."

His comment was so ironic and unexpected, Jenna

laughed. "I never strived to be queen of anything. As for mountains, I'd say this one conquered us, not the other way around." She stared at him for a moment. "You really have a warped view."

"Must be all the thin air I breathe."

She chuckled even as she shook her head. "I never thought I'd actually laugh at dumb tall jokes." She looked up to the sky. "Jenna King, you've finally hit bottom."

"No, we did that about a half hour ago."

It was his straight face that set her off. "Enough," she finally said, pressing her sides as she continued to laugh.

She leaned back against the tree when he laid his head on the ground. She was wet, hurt, stranded, with little hope of rescue. So why was she almost enjoying herself? She frowned.

"I don't buy it," he said.

Startled, she looked at him. Realizing he couldn't have read her mind, she asked, "Don't buy what?"

"That you have no royal aspirations."

"What are you talking about?" Maybe he really had hit his head. Then it sank in. "Oh, being queen you mean." She snorted. "Trust me, my goal in life has never been to be the center of attention. At six-two it isn't easy to blend in, but I've done a damn good job of it."

He looked at her. "You? Blend in? I don't think so. And before you get all defensive on me, I'm not talking about your height. I wasn't before either. When I said I'd never met anyone like you, I was referring to character, not physical attributes." He glanced down at himself. "I'd be the last person to comment on size."

Knowing she shouldn't but too curious not to, she asked, "What's so unique about my character?"

"You're probably the most stubborn, determined person I've ever met. And if you knew the crew I work with, you'd realize that's really saying something."

"I'd rather not know what," she said dryly.

"I meant that as a compliment."

"Compliment? Gee, stop now, you'll swell my head. And I'm swollen enough, thank you."

He chuckled, then winced. She straightened and started to shift her ankle off of him, but he lifted a hand. "No, don't move it."

Her response was automatic. "How badly are you hurt? You banged yourself up pretty good. Did you check for cuts?"

"I don't feel anything warm or sticky. I think the cold and the rain has closed whatever scrapes I do have."

"You should let me take a look. I'm not a nurse, but I am trained to—" Jenna froze. Her automatic reaction was far from reassuring. *What was she doing?*

Caring.

No. Uh-uh. She couldn't afford to care. Not even superficially. That was the only sure way she knew of to avoid ever again having to face the consequences. One lesson life—or more to the point, death—had taught her was that there were always consequences to caring. And they were always negative.

She quickly recovered. "It wouldn't do any good. There isn't anything to clean them out with anyway."

"You're trained to what, Jenna? What do you do that's not being a nurse?" His tone was casual. His expression was anything but.

She told herself to remember that. He might be big and friendly, but he was no overgrown puppy dog. *So what was he?* How had he gotten injured? What crew did he work for? She tamped down her curiosity. Curiosity led to questions, questions led to sharing, sharing led to friendship, and friendship meant caring. And she knew somewhere deep down in a resolutely unexplored part of her soul that she could care about this man.

"I don't do anything," she said, proud of the steel thread she'd managed to keep in her voice.

He didn't even pause. "Sure you do. For one thing, you hike."

Was he making small talk? She didn't think so. For an affable sort, he had a remarkable ability to focus. And right now he was intently focused on her. "I obviously don't hike well."

"On the contrary, I'd bet you have quite a bit of experience."

Her eyes narrowed, but she forced a smile, though it was a dry one. "What gave me away? My high-tech backpack or my rappelling capabilities?" Too late she realized she'd handed him an even more dangerous topic.

"Actually I was referring to the way you handled the situation. You didn't panic. You maneuvered up that rocky ravine with a bum ankle without so much as a groan."

Jenna sighed inwardly in relief. He'd overlooked the backpack. "I didn't see where I had a choice. Trust me, on the inside I was swearing like a sailor. Some people appear calmer in certain situations. Like you. You even joked about it."

"Some people use humor to deflect fear," he responded.

The glint in his eye and the reappearance of his dimples told her he was teasing. "Oh yeah, I'm sure you were terrified."

The glint hardened a bit. "Size and fear aren't always mutually exclusive."

There was no avoiding the hot blush that colored her cheeks. "I seem to be putting my foot in my mouth regularly today."

"Must hurt your ankle like hell," he shot back.

She fell silent, confused by the nuances of his personality that she hadn't anticipated. The emotions he unleashed in her confused her even more, emotions she'd just as soon keep buried. Deeply buried.

"You ever been afraid, Jenna? I mean truly terrified?"

His question took her off guard. Without warning, horrific images invaded her mind. In a wave of heat and color, a voracious wall of fire roared toward her, consuming ground cover, trees—her crew. She squeezed her eyes shut, but it kept coming. She put her hands over her ears, but it did nothing to block out the incredible whooshing roar. Nor did it silence the screams of her men.

T.J. watched as what little color there was in her damp cheeks washed swiftly out, leaving her dangerously pale. "Jenna, I'm sorry. Jenna." She'd closed her eyes and covered her ears. She didn't hear him. "Jenna!"

Dear God, what had he made her recall? He'd had no way of knowing he'd trigger something horrific, but there was no doubt that he had. His knee argued against his moving, but he didn't care. Careful not to dislodge her ankle from his thigh, he slid closer and touched her arm. His shoulder ached, but he ignored it. He couldn't let her endure this agony alone one second longer.

He took hold of her forearm and gently tugged. "Jenna. Jenna, listen to me. Listen!" The sudden vehement order had the desired effect. Her head shot up and she stared at him, unseeing. He cupped her cheek and turned her head until her eyes were aimed right at his. "Look at me," he directed in the same "do it now" tone of command. "Look at me." Slowly her focus shifted outward. "You're okay," he said, his voice calmer but still laced with steel. "There is no danger here. You're safe." She finally looked at him, and what he saw in that unguarded moment broke his heart.

Something had terrorized her beyond the endurance of her defenses and continued to ravage her still. He already knew her to be a proud, strong woman.

He didn't want to imagine what it had taken to reduce her to this state.

Still staring at him, her expression like one of shell shock, she started to shake.

"Oh baby," he said under his breath. He stroked her cheek. It was still cold and far too pale. "It's okay, Jenna," he said, knowing that whatever had happened to her was far from okay. Keeping his voice as soft and soothing as he could make it, he continued to reassure her, to stroke her. She was still staring through him, still shaking.

Very carefully, he reached down and gently slid her foot from his thigh to the ground. She didn't even blink.

"Come here, Jenna."

Confusion briefly flitted through her empty expression.

"Come here," he said softly, and pulled at her arm.

"I couldn't stop it," she said, her tone as lifeless as her gaze. "I tried but I—" She broke off on a low moan, moving her head back and forth as her shaking increased until her teeth chattered with it.

T.J. didn't wait for permission, he acted on instinct. If she fought him, they'd both pay, but he risked it without hesitation. He pulled her sideways and down until they were both on their sides. She didn't fight until he wrapped his arm around her waist and tried to pull her into his arms.

"Don't hit my knee."

The unexpected directive worked, making her

pause for a second. He took advantage of the moment and tucked her head into the curve of his shoulder. He pressed his mouth to the soft spot below her ear and spoke softly. "Don't fight me, I won't hurt you. Lie here and rest. It's okay to rest here, Jenna." When he felt her head relax, he shifted his hand to her back and began a series of long, slow strokes. "Shhh, it's going to be okay." He wished he were certain of that. He'd witnessed terror and endured torture and had both a healthy respect and a deep-seated hatred of the power the two wielded on the human psyche.

He wanted not only to protect her, but to destroy the cause of her fear. He had no explanation for the ferocity of his feelings, but he didn't question them either. He also didn't question the knowledge that if he let it, this anger, this need he felt could consume him.

His hands stilled for a moment, then he continued his quiet words and gentle touches, breathing a sigh of his own as her shaking gradually diminished.

Her body grew heavier, and her head began to loll as sleep overtook her. He silently prayed that the nightmare he'd unknowingly sprung on her wouldn't stalk her into sleep. But she rested peacefully against him.

Pain jabbed viciously at his knee. He shifted slightly so he could look down at her. His pain didn't diminish one iota, but he was suddenly less cognizant of it. He stroked one finger along the side of her face.

It was still too pale and felt cool and clammy under his touch. He looked at her closed eyes, the thick lashes wet and spiky against her cheeks, and pictured the brown eyes hidden beneath. In his mind's eye he watched them change, remembered the horror and anguish he'd seen there before they'd become lifeless and empty.

I couldn't stop it.

What? he wondered. Had she hurt her ankle trying to save something, someone? Was the guilt her failure had burdened her with all self-imposed?

He stroked a finger along her jaw and stared at her lips. They were full and wide, a natural deep red that looked even richer now against her pale skin. A tiny smile curved his lips. She had a mouth on her too. His throat suddenly clutched, and his smile faded as he acknowledged how badly he wanted to taste that smart mouth.

He looked down the length of their bodies and his need escalated.

She fit him. It was as simple as that and as complex.

She had strength, both physical and mental. Her body was long, lean, and more hard than soft, which made the soft places she did have all the more erotic.

Maybe it was the combination of her obvious strengths and her well-hidden, but definite vulnerabilities that got to him.

He looked once again at her closed eyes and traced her eyebrows lightly, then he gave in to temptation and lightly brushed his fingertip along the fringe of her eyelashes.

"Whatever it is, Jenna King," he whispered, "you make me want to slay dragons for you."

He slowly lowered his head to the ground and tucked hers more closely against him. He'd like nothing more than to wrap his arms and body around her, to hold her as tightly as he could. She did fit him, in so many ways, and it was frustrating in the extreme not to be able to indulge in that experience. Her damp hair tickled his nose. He buried it deeper.

Patience, he thought as his eyes drifted shut. He tucked his arm more securely around her back. *Patience.*

It was the screaming that woke them up.

Jenna was already sitting up, wide-eyed with sleepy confusion, before she realized she'd just pulled herself from T. J. Delahaye's most accommodating embrace. That more than anything brought her quickly and widely awake.

The scream came again.

T.J. rolled to his back, then froze. He swore under his breath, and Jenna knew he'd cramped up from lying on the damp ground.

"What in the hell is that?" he said through clenched teeth.

"Whatever it is, it's in pain," Jenna replied as calmly as possible. Inside her head was chaos. *Not again, please not again. Hasn't there been enough misery for one day?* It was a useless query. The strange wail echoed again.

T.J. was slowly rearranging his body so he was flat on his back. Jenna very carefully looked away. The ground was still cold and damp, but her cheeks, hands, chest, and belly were warm. She knew the source of that warmth was the man stretched beside her. She was almost thankful for the continued wailing, as it prevented her from having to think back on how she'd ended up asleep in his arms.

"It's not human," she said, scanning the land along the side of the ravine. The pine trees formed a thick stand that ran parallel to it. She could see a good distance down the stretch of land that ran between, but there was no sign of anything unusual, man or beast. "I think it's coming from back there somewhere," she said, pointing into the trees at their right side.

The wail echoed again, sounding like part bleat, part growl. "Something caught in the flash flood, you think? I saw from the trail up there that there are small creeks and streams running all through here."

Jenna shivered lightly. "We're lucky this whole area didn't end up underwater."

The wail erupted yet again. She rubbed her arms. It was selfish in the extreme, but she wasn't sure how long she could take listening to whatever it was suffer. Sleep had helped her regain some energy, but had done next to nothing to help her sort out her mental problems.

"I doubt it's a wildcat," T.J. said. "The noise would be ten times worse."

Jenna doubted that was possible, but she refrained from commenting. She remembered most of what had happened earlier despite her efforts to block it out. She did block out the nightmare part, at least. The part that involved sleeping in T.J.'s arms was proving a bit harder to ignore. She knew it was exhaustion, both mental and physical, that had caused her to react the way she had. At least that's what she was telling herself.

He probably thought she was a total fruitcake.

Right now what T.J. Delahaye thought of her was the least of her concerns. She should be thankful for the distraction. For once, he wasn't asking questions.

The scream came again, and she swore out loud. It took more willpower than she liked to admit to keep from clapping her hands over her ears. "Whatever the hell it is, I wish it would stop."

"Yeah, I know what you mean."

His response surprised her, even comforted her a tiny bit. Maybe she was normal after all, she thought. Anyone would react the same after what she'd been through. But the fingernails she was digging into her sock-wrapped palms put the lie to her reassurances.

"It's hell not being able to do anything to help the poor thing," T.J. said.

Jenna stilled. Help it? As in rescue? *Dear God, no.*

"Maybe if I—"

She swung her gaze to his, hating the fear that balled up in the pit of her stomach. "Maybe if you what, Delahaye? You can't even stand up." He raised an eyebrow at the vehemence in her tone but didn't look away. Don't look at me like that, she wanted to demand. Don't challenge me. You don't know what you're asking.

As if to underscore his patient stare, the wail changed to a low keening sound.

She swore under her breath. "I guess if anyone is going to find out what's going on, it'll have to be me."

"You're not in much better shape. Your ankle—"

"Is in better shape than your knee." She stared right back at him. "We can't sit here and let it suffer, isn't that what you said?"

"No, it isn't."

She ignored him. It was his fault she had to take action. It had to be his fault. Without anger—specifically anger focused at someone other than herself—she wasn't sure she could pull it off. *That way, if you fail, it will be his fault too?*

"Shut up," she mumbled to herself. She spied a branch she could use for a crutch and began scooting toward it, pushing with her good foot.

"Jenna, wait a minute. Slow down here."

She was already looking for another broken branch strong enough to support her weight. Her ankle was banged up and her leg was tight and unhappy, but the terrain was relatively even. She could do this.

She had no choice.

She simply could not survive being put through

the emotional grind of helplessly listening to another living thing dying a slow, agonizing death.

Thankful for the socks padding her palms, she grabbed the branch and levered to a stand, refusing to consider what she would do if she failed once again.

FIVE

"Jenna!" T.J. watched as she hobbled toward the denser part of the bordering forest. She turned inward and was swallowed up by the centuries-old pines. He slapped the ground. "Damn her stubborn hide to hell." His frustration was doubled by the fact that he wasn't exactly in prime condition to race after her.

There was no telling what she'd find out there. Wild animals weren't always predictable. Wounded wild animals never were. Jenna wasn't stupid, but she wasn't thinking clearly either.

There had been a flash of pure terror on her face when he'd mentioned helping the poor creature. Yet less than five seconds later, despite his warnings, she was storming off to save the damn thing as if it were her personal mission in life. Every time he thought he was closer to figuring out another piece of her puzzle, the piece would elude him.

She'd told him she was from Paradise Canyon, he assumed to rehab her ankle, yet he'd found her stranded on the side of a mountain with all her personal belongings strapped to her back in a laundry bag. She seemed quite capable and confident about handling herself in the wilderness, but she had no gear and no clear destination or means to get there. She displayed a deep core of inner strength, yet she was haunted by something that terrified her.

One thing was clear. Something was driving Jenna King, and T.J. was very much afraid that whatever it was had taken her right to the edge. He felt responsible for her current state, even though he'd had no way of knowing his concern would set her off.

I couldn't stop it.

Her anguished words echoed in his mind. He muttered another curse. *Stupid, Delahaye. Really stupid.*

She'd taken his concern for the animal as a challenge. He didn't know the source of her demons—yet—but one of them was definitely guilt. And he'd aimed her right at it.

Jenna paused and leaned against the trunk of a mighty Douglas fir. At any other time she would have taken a moment to absorb the power and beauty of her surroundings. Some of the trees were over eight hundred years old. But right now she was focused on the sound of pain.

And the feel of it. Her ankle was screaming. Gravity was wreaking havoc on the swelling. Holding her foot up was excruciating.

Despite the earlier rain, the entire area was seriously parched. Wildfires had ravaged the West all summer long, some still burned in southern California due to the dry, hot Santa Ana winds. Fire season was usually over by now in the north, but the unseasonably warm fall had kept firefighters busy. She looked around her. These magnificent trees represented some of the oldest growth in the country. And all this underbrush was a torch begging to be lit. One lightning strike and—

Like the wail of a siren, the keening noise suddenly rose to a high pitch, eerily underscoring the abruptly increased speed of her pulse. Shutting out any and all thoughts of forest fires, she once again moved toward the wounded animal.

Jenna knew enough about the area in general to have a good idea of what species of animals were likely to roam wild. And the sound she was hearing couldn't be matched to any of them.

The high pitch lowered back down, the wail rougher and not as strong. She knew the fading sound meant the animal was growing weaker, not that she was heading away from it. The forest was no longer her "office," but her sense of direction was still solid. She knew she was headed in the right direction, just as she knew she could navigate directly back to T.J.

His handsome face immediately flashed through her mind. He hadn't been smiling when she'd left. In fact, she might have thought twice about going if she hadn't been certain he couldn't stop her on his own. The total assurance in his voice had surprised her. She'd seen a glimmer of it in his eyes, heard it thread through his deceptively soft, rumbling voice, but never had she expected such absolute command. He'd barked an order and had expected immediate compliance. It was obviously not the first time. She'd discovered another intriguing facet to him that tempted her curiosity.

"Damn the man," she said softly. She didn't want to care. She didn't want him to make her wonder about him. But she had no idea how to keep him from doing so. By simply losing his temper, he revealed parts of himself to her she had no desire to know about. Dangerous parts.

She was beginning to realize that there wasn't anything about T. J. Delahaye that wasn't dangerous.

So don't go back. Go get help instead.

She stopped cold. She had to go back. Didn't she?

The highway she'd been headed for originally was completely out of reach now. She closed her eyes and visualized the map she'd studied at Paradise. There weren't many main roads in this part of Jackson County, but there were back roads. And back roads led to main roads.

This was insane. She couldn't just leave T.J. there. He'd be worried sick. But he wouldn't die of worry, she countered. And it wasn't as if he could go anywhere or do anything to hurt himself further. He was stuck right where he was until help came.

"And once again, you're elected." She sighed

heavily. Talk about the lesser of two evils. Yes, he'd be angry and upset, but he'd be rescued. And she wouldn't have to deal with him again.

It occurred to her that she wasn't certain she could make it to a road. In her current condition, it would take hours. Possibly longer.

And if you don't make it? She rubbed her arms and pushed away the nerve-destroying images that always seemed to haunt the fringes of her mind, waiting for even the tiniest sign that she'd relaxed her vigilant control so they could pounce on her. But what other options did she have?

If she'd had a chance to talk it over with T.J., surely they'd have come to the same conclusion.

Jenna knew damn well T.J. would never have let her go off alone in search of help, but he hadn't "let" her go this time either. She should be feeling good about taking control of the situation, taking charge of the events that shaped her life instead of the other way around.

So why did she feel as if she was about to make her biggest mistake yet?

A sharp bleat followed by a gurgling growl jerked her from her thoughts. She bit off a curse. She'd forgotten to include the damned animal in her big plan.

She was close now, within a hundred yards or so, by her estimate. She had to find it, see what was wrong, see if there was anything she could do to ease its suffering.

She felt the stirrings of a shiver begin deep inside her and immediately intensified her focus, knowing if she let go now, the ball of fear churning inside her would take over and paralyze her. Then they would all die.

Wedging the knobby ends of the broken branches under her arms, she continued to work her way through the brush toward the sound.

Less than five minutes later the forest ended abruptly. So did her search.

"What in the hell is that?" she muttered, then went silent and still as she took in the rest of the scenery.

She hung back between the last line of trees and surveyed the situation. Twenty yards below, down a relatively smooth slope, a narrow valley spread out before her. The tree line was a good quarter mile up, the land below was a charred graveyard of tree stubs.

Fire had struck here. She clamped down on the queasiness that pitched in her stomach and forced herself to focus on the remains in an objective manner. The fire had happened this season, a few months earlier at best. Her hands shook slightly, and her forehead beaded with sweat that made her feel cold and clammy, but she continued to scan the damage. She forced a slow breath in then back out before turning away.

A small creek bed freshly swollen by the rain wended its way through the valley floor. It had likely been what had saved the forest on her side.

Unfortunately, the creature now stuck in the oozing silt and muck left behind as the waters receded hadn't received the same protection.

The animal was lying down, its head tucked low and turned away from her. The blackish-brown, sticky-looking silt and ash mud that matted its clumpy hair made it impossible to identify. Its body was the size of a large dog, but its legs, what she could see of them all mired in the muck, were long and slender. A young mule deer maybe? She stepped from the trees as it swung up a long graceful neck, tilted its little head back, and let out a mournful howl that had her murmuring, "Poor baby," without being aware of it.

"Of all things," she said, frowning. A baby llama.

Jenna shook her head and focused on navigating the gentle slope on her makeshift crutches, but stopped when the howl turned to frantic bleats. It had seen her and was now renewing its struggle to get free, trying to get to its feet and lurching dangerously back, going deeper into the black mud with each attempt.

"Shhh, it's okay," she called out, trying to keep her tone soothing but loud enough to be heard. She redoubled her efforts, moving as fast as she could. The animal was exhausted, and she was afraid it would hurt itself. It took another ten minutes or so, but she finally got within five feet. If she moved any closer, she risked getting stuck right alongside the damn thing.

"How in the world did you get way out here all by yourself, you silly beast?" she said, her tone sweet and gentle despite her words. The llama stopped struggling.

A long, fuzzy camellike nose swung in her direction, and she found herself looking into impossibly soulful black eyes fringed with the thickest, longest lashes she'd ever seen.

"You stupid sweetie," she crooned. "I bet you're exhausted, aren't you?" Its ears came forward, alert to her voice. It continued to stay still, so she kept talking, all the while wondering what in the hell she was going to do.

She'd never been around llamas before, but it was common knowledge that they had grown in popularity as pets and were also used as pack animals by hiking outfitters. She knew llama ranching had become a viable industry. This one apparently had wandered off, or its owner's ranch might have been destroyed in the recent wildfire.

The baby didn't look newborn, but it probably was at the time of the fire. Where was the mother?

She swallowed hard as her stomach pitched again. *Concentrate on getting this thing loose.*

"Yeah, and then what?" she grumbled. The llama continued to stare, its only reply a slow, long-lashed blink. "Thanks," she said dryly, but she couldn't help the smile that teased the corner of her mouth. "You really are a pitiful thing, aren't you?" Another blink. "At least you know when to keep your mouth shut."

It leaned toward her, extending its long neck as far as it could go. Jenna stilled, then took a careful step forward and leaned on one crutch as she bent over and reached out to its soft, fuzzy muzzle. It sniffed at the sock wrapped around her hand as Jenna lightly stroked it. The baby curled the flappy sides of its mouth back, revealing blocky white lower teeth. The resulting expression was an incredibly goofy-looking grin.

Jenna laughed and stroked it again, surprised and oddly moved when her efforts were rewarded with a rumbling hum inside its long throat. The baby pushed its nose harder against Jenna's hand and the hum deepened. "You sound like a big cat," she said, delighted despite her stern determination to remain unaffected. The baby grinned again. Her heart was gone.

"What am I going to do with you?"

"Save her."

Jenna shrieked at the unexpected deep voice. A second later she joined the baby llama in the mud. Frightened, the baby reared back, splattering black ashy muck all over Jenna's shirt and face.

Scraping at the goo, Jenna swung her narrowed gaze back around. "Delahaye! How in the hell did you get—"

"Duck!" T.J. ordered, cutting her off.

Jenna turned back to the llama, raising her arm up to ward off the unforeseen threat. The baby had straightened its neck, aimed its head upward, and flattened his ears. Jenna lowered her arm, once again turning to T.J. "What? It's scared and you yelling at me isn't helping. I don't think it'll bite—"

"No, but it will—"

There was a guttural sound followed by a warm, wet splat as a glob of something grossly foul smelling hit the back of her shirt.

"Spit," T.J. finished, grinning unrepentantly.

"Oh, disgusting!" She looked at the baby reprovingly. "Is that any way to treat your rescuer?" The baby's ears went forward again as it lowered its head, looked at her, and blinked. "Apology not accepted," Jenna said crossly, but her tone was gentle. She sat stiffly. "Oh, this is so gross." It was all she could do not to yank the now rank garment off her body. Modesty didn't stop her—fear of smearing the spit did. "I ought to leave you here."

"Same thing is crossing my mind."

She didn't look at him. Her cheeks had flushed as guilt crept through her. He might be teasing, but she'd seriously planned to leave him. "Yeah, he's some invalid, Jenna," she muttered under her breath.

"What was that?"

Without turning, she raised her voice. "I said fine, leave me here. I don't think I can survive another one of your rescue attempts."

The baby shifted nervously at her tone. Not wanting another spit grenade, Jenna quickly reached out a tentative hand. After a cursory sniff, the baby pushed its face closer. Jenna opted for stroking its long neck. "Just don't breathe on me, okay?"

"She likes you," T.J. said.

Jenna snorted. "Yeah, right. I'm sure she spits on all of her friends. What makes you so sure it's a female?"

"Just guessing. Can't be much more than five or six months old."

The rumbling purr returned as she continued to

stroke the baby. "Brat," she said, fighting a smile even as the noxious spit fumes continued their assault on her olfactory senses.

"Want some help?" he offered.

A smart retort was on the tip of her tongue, when she finally remembered to wonder how in the hell he'd gotten there. Continuing to pet the baby, she finally shifted around to face him.

Her mouth fell open. Her throat dried up. It was the first time she'd seen him upright. Standing there in dirt-streaked, torn-up blue jeans, hiking boots, wild wet hair, and a bare chest the size of Mount Rushmore, he looked like the centerfold of *Lumberjack Monthly*.

The fact that he'd fashioned a crude brace for his knee out of broken branches and torn shirt strips and was leaning heavily on a gnarly-looking tree-limb crutch did nothing to diminish the aura of raw power he emanated. It rolled off of him in waves.

His sexy grin knocked the power up a few hundred volts. "Yeah, I know. I'm not much of a bargain."

She was tempted to deny his assessment vigorously, but her sanity was mercifully restored when he continued.

"But I'm all you've got."

"Thanks, I think I'll take my chances with the baby."

He tried to look offended. The dimples blew it. "I may not be in great shape, but at least I don't spit."

Why her mind chose that moment to recall the

feel of his broad chest, all warm against her cheek, or those boulder-size arms wrapped firmly but gently around her she had no idea, but she didn't appreciate it. The image wasn't so easy to block out this time. Staring at him wasn't helping, but she couldn't seem to look away. "I can handle it," she told him, not remotely sure of any such thing.

Being one of only a handful of female smoke jumpers in the country, she'd come across as many wild men as wildfires. But T. J. Delahaye was in a class all by himself. The man looked as if he could stomp out fires. Barefoot.

"Like I said, stubborn and determined."

She scowled and looked away, scanning the mud for her makeshift crutches. With a final pat to the baby's head, she worked to unearth the branches from the muck.

Careful to move slowly so as not to alarm the baby, she half clawed, half dragged her backside, thighs, and one foot out of the deepest part of the mud, but her other foot and bad ankle were pushed in too deep. She was going to have to pull hard to get it out. It was going to hurt like hell, and possibly injure her further, but she had no choice. There was no use trying to dig out, the mud would ooze right back in. Clamping her jaw, she tried, then tried again. By the fourth time she mentally concluded that the mud was going to win, unless she asked for help.

T.J. might tease her, but stubborn and determined had gotten her a long way in life. They'd get her out of this mess.

"Take off your shirt."

Surprised by the proximity of his voice, she turned her head. He was only a few feet behind her, at the edge where the scrub brush turned to mud and silt. He moved quietly for a big man, a big *injured* man. God, but the man was truly a giant.

The heat was back again, all dark and warm and tempting. There was no use denying the man caused an elemental reaction in her.

Somewhat unwillingly, she pulled her gaze to his. "I beg your pardon?"

"The only way to get you out of here is to sit behind you so you can grab onto me, use me for leverage. I'd pull you out, but I can't bend my knee."

"What does that have to do with me stripping?"

"Well, I like you and all, Jenna, but I'd as soon not swap llama spit with you." He nodded at her shirt. "If you know what I mean."

Eyebrows raised, Jenna looked at him and laughed. "Paul Bunyan afraid of a little muck and mire? You obviously haven't looked in a mirror lately."

He leaned on his makeshift crutches and lifted one hand, palm up. "Hey, mud and dirt are one thing—"

"And blood and gravel and grass. Come on, Delahaye, I may be afraid of some things, but a little ash, dirt, and muck are hardly worth worrying about. I've spent half my life covered by one or all three of them. Surely a big guy like you can handle a little spit." She wanted nothing more than to tear the offensive thing off of her, but ribbing T.J. felt too good.

The sun chose that moment to emerge from the last remaining storm clouds, lighting T.J.'s blue eyes with a crystal gleam. "That's not a *little* spit. It's green, Jenna."

"Oh, gross!" She sat up straighter and held out her arms, as if that might separate her even marginally from the slime.

He laughed. "It's just a little spit," he mimicked.

"That was more information than I needed to know, okay?"

He moved closer, and Jenna noted he was leaning very heavily on his crutches. Despite his good-natured teasing, which she suspected he'd keep up even under torture, he was likely in substantial pain. "You should be sitting down with that knee immobilized."

"I'd like nothing better, so stop whining and take your shirt off. You've got more than one on."

Yes, she did. But that was all she had on. And both her long underwear and her henley were soaking wet. Suddenly she could feel every soaking-wet inch of her waffle-knit shirt clinging to every damp inch of her skin. Her nipples peaked. And it had nothing whatsoever to do with being cold and wet.

Modesty, Jenna? Maybe it wasn't the spit after all. The idea confounded her. She'd spent the major part of her life surrounded by men, doing a job that required living in a dormitory existence that demanded a certain lack of modesty in order for them all to perform their duties. But that had been under harsh, emergency situations, she reasoned, conveniently forgetting the hours of boredom smoke jumpers were forced to deal with in between assignments. Where had her modesty been then?

She looked away, wiping her suddenly warm cheeks on her shoulder, carefully avoiding looking at the fire-charred mountainside. She looked instead past the baby, downstream into the narrow valley.

She hadn't felt modesty because the subject had never come up. She'd made damn sure the men treated her as a firefighter first, last, and always. And they had. She'd told herself it was necessary to ensure their respect and maintain professionalism. Not an easy task. But now she wondered if that's all she'd been ensuring.

"Jenna?"

The teasing voice was gone, replaced by one filled with concern. Caring.

She straightened her shoulders and carefully pulled one arm, then the other, inside her shirt, then eased the sodden fabric as carefully over her head as she could. It wasn't until she held the torn muddy mess in her hands that she smiled, then laughed.

"What's so funny?"

I'm a fool, that's what. She tossed the shirt on the opposite side of the streambed. A man had finally managed to get past her defenses, get her hormones all stirred up, and get her worrying about things like wet, nipple-clinging shirts and bare breasts and modesty. . . . And she was sitting in a streambed covered in soot and ash and muck—and llama spit. *Oh yeah, Jenna, better not let him see your nipples, you'll send the man over the edge with lust for sure.*

"Nothing," she said, a dry smile still curving her lips. He edged closer, and her smile faded abruptly as her body reacted to him, to his proximity. Damn the man. Damn her. She might not inspire lust, but he had. She did not want his hands on her. She felt foolish enough as it was.

"You know—" The words got all tangled up somehow, sounding deep and even rougher than usual. Still not looking at him, she cleared her throat. "With the sun out, this mud ought to dry up fairly quickly. I don't want you to risk hurting your knee any further. Why don't you rest. I'll work my way out."

There was a long pause. She felt his gaze on her. Never had she been more aware of herself. What was he thinking as he looked at her?

"What about the baby?"

He was thinking about the llama. She sighed. *Reality check, Jenna*. "I can help her too." She reached out to pet the baby's nose. The llama had been quiet, seemingly content as long as Jenna stayed nearby and didn't raise her voice.

She stiffened as the ground vibrated behind her and long legs slowly slid on either side of hers. She would have turned, but strong hands had clamped on her sides. She looked down to see his long fingers spread across her stomach beneath her breasts. Tanned and dirty, they made a stark contrast to her cream-colored shirt, as did the dark hue of her nipples as they strained against the wet fabric.

She opened her mouth to tell him what he could

do and where he could go do it, but found her breath had vanished.

"You—you're getting my shirt dirty," she managed to mumble, her gaze still riveted to those fingers. Her breasts ached. She ached.

His voice was a velvet whisper in her ear. "Afraid of getting a little messy, Jenna?"

SIX

Damn but she felt good. It was all he could do not to press his lips against the skin below her ear. T.J. chuckled when she stiffened further at his whispered words.

"Ready?" He took her silence as a yes. She was a handful in more ways than one. And he quite liked having his hands full of Jenna King. "Hold on to my arms and use me for leverage."

"You can't anchor your leg any better than I could. We'll both slide in."

"I'm not going anywhere. Hold on and pull."

She didn't respond for several seconds, then gradually she relaxed and redirected her strength. Her trust, however tentative, warmed him more than the sun now beating down on his back. He felt the slight relaxation of her lower back, the increasing tension across her shoulders and neck as she got ready to pull once again. But when she carefully took hold of his arms, he wasn't expecting the sharp response of his body. A small moan escaped him before he could stop it.

She stiffened all over again, dropping his arms. "What's wrong? I told you you shouldn't do this."

"It's okay," he lied. Okay right now would be closing the scant distance between her sweet backside and the tight bulge threatening the seam of his jeans. Okay would be pulling her fully into his arms and working on assuaging this craving he'd somehow managed to develop. He wasn't sure even that would be enough. "Come on," he said, his tone a bit harsher than he'd intended.

She hadn't missed it either. She turned her head and pulled back a little so she could see him. "T.J., I can get out of here on my own. I appreciate the help, but it won't do either of us any good if you injure yourself further." A dry smile kicked at the corners of her mouth. "Trust me, I'm one woman you don't have to impress with macho maneuvers."

He tore his gaze from her lips. He was certain kissing her right then would rate worse than rescuing her on the macho-maneuver scale. He'd rather risk injury.

"I wasn't trying to impress you. I was trying to help."

"Yes, I know. You don't really make a living at that, do you?"

"Very funny." If there'd been a gun aimed at his head, he couldn't have looked away from her then. For the first time her smile reached her eyes, warming them, lighting them with vibrancy . . . with life. He hadn't realized how empty they'd truly been until now. He reached up and tucked one of the drying wispy tendrils behind her ear. "You have a beautiful smile, Jenna King. You should wear it more often."

Just like that, the life winked out of her eyes. She turned away, her back to him once again. He regretted his lack of finesse, but he wasn't going to back away this time. There had been a blink of vulnerability in her expression before anger had shut all other emotion down. He imagined that anger was quite effective in helping her close people out.

He ignored her anger and focused on the other glimpse of her—the real her—he'd seen. "I'm sorry if getting compliments bothers you, but I won't apologize for giving you one. I wasn't trying to impress, I wasn't trying anything. I was speaking the truth as I saw it. You have a beautiful smile. Especially when it reaches your eyes."

"Thank you," she said stiffly. "Now let's get out of here."

"That doesn't happen often, does it, Jenna?" He didn't expect an answer, and she didn't disappoint him. "I'm sorry for that. Sorry for whatever keeps you from smiling." T.J. sighed, but placed his hands firmly on her hips. "Grab on." Even though he'd been prepared for it, her touch still jolted him. His fingertips tingled beneath her breasts, and he found himself staring at the heavy braid that lay along the slender line of her neck. He wanted to press closer, feel it brush his skin. Admiring her strong shoulders, he held the proof of her narrow waist in his hands. She jolted him all right.

"My foot is anchored," she said.

"On three," he said. "One . . . two . . . three."

He felt her strong grip on his arms as she pressed herself back. She was grunting under the strain, and he felt her begin to slip forward. He held her tighter as a loud sucking noise erupted from the muck in front of them. When her foot popped free, the sudden shift in balance shoved her backward on top of him.

She quickly rolled off of him, sending a spasm through him that he was helpless to hide.

She pushed upright and scooted up alongside him. He opened his eyes to find her staring down at him, her expression part anxious, part furious. He focused on the former.

"I'm okay," he lied.

"You're anything but okay."

Thrashing sounds got both of their attention, and they turned to find the baby llama renewing her struggle.

"Shh, *cria*," T.J. crooned. "It's okay, baby. It'll be okay." He turned back to Jenna, whose expression now included confusion and curiosity. *Good*, he thought, *now I'm not alone*. "Go soothe her, she seems to listen to you."

She stared at him for a second, questions clear in her eyes, but silently did as he asked, scooting along the edge of the muddy streambed to get as close to the baby as she could without getting stuck again.

"It's okay. Calm down," she said. The baby struggled for a few more seconds, but Jenna continued to talk to her, and eventually the llama quieted and turned her head, looking straight at Jenna.

T.J. watched her along with the exhausted, frightened animal. She was a woman with a strict rule of self-reliance, yet there was no denying that gentility and compassion were also a natural part of her. He wondered again what had happened to her to make her work so hard at stifling her softer side. "You have a way with animals," he said.

"Good thing my folks aren't here to hear you say that," she said somewhat distractedly. She was looking around, probably trying to figure out some way to get the baby loose.

T.J. weighed the wisdom of following up on that tantalizing bit of personal information, but finally figured he had nothing to lose by asking. "Your parents don't like animals?"

She stilled, but only for a second. He sensed she'd spoken without thinking and would pull back now. He was surprised when she answered.

Looking back at the baby, she said, "Quite the opposite. They breed horses and range some cattle. Then there's the chickens and goats, a few sheep last I heard, the barn cats who manage to keep the haylofts filled with kittens, and a farm dog or three."

"I take it ranching isn't your goal in life."

She shook her head and blew out a short breath. "You take it right. I ride okay, but running a ranch was not something I ever yearned to do."

Before he could ask what she did yearn for, the baby began wiggling again, the slowly drying ground giving it a bit more traction this time. T.J. braced himself to get up in case Jenna needed him, but the baby settled back down as soon as she had accomplished her goal: getting closer to Jenna. T.J. smiled and tucked his arm behind his head, watching as Jenna edged closer until she could reach out and touch the baby's muzzle again.

"Careful," he warned. "I'm not sure I'm up to getting you out of there again."

"And here I thought you lived to rescue." Her expression remained soft as she continued to look at and stroke the baby. "Spit on me again, you big overgrown sheep, and you're on your own," she said, her voice every bit as gentle as her smile.

T.J. chuckled. There might be more soft edges to Jenna than he'd thought, but she'd never go completely soft on him. A sigh whispered out of him, and he relaxed back on the ground, the image of Jenna going all soft on him—and under him—filling his mind. Lord, what a tantalizing mix her strength and softness would make. Untamed. Raw. Wild. Those were the words that came to mind when he thought about what making love with Jenna King would be like. Evenly matched. Oh yes, that too. In body and in spirit.

He closed his eyes, but the images remained, as he knew his craving for Jenna would remain. He grew hard again. It was an additional ache he didn't need right now. "So your parents wanted you to take on the family business?"

Prodding her in the hope that she'd go all stiff and quiet and shove that wedge back between them was not a noble route for him to take. He wasn't happy with himself, but he had to survive this too.

"Actually, that was my older brother's burden. Not that he would have minded. He loved ranching. It was in his blood. I left as soon as I could."

Again, she surprised him. His reaction did too. He was intrigued and not remotely disappointed that she'd opted for more talk instead of clamming up on him again. He lifted his head in time to catch the flicker of pain that flashed across her face, taking her smile with it when it fled. Her expression was carefully neutral now. She continued to stroke the baby.

T.J. wasn't sure what to do. He felt worse now about prodding her. He didn't want to upset her. For reasons he didn't examine too closely, it was very important to him not to be another person in her life who caused her pain.

He suspected she didn't confide in many people, if anyone. It had to be difficult for her to do so now. Why him? he wondered. He doubted it was because he'd inspired any great devotion on her part. She'd made it more than clear what she thought of his rescuing abilities. Maybe she'd felt safer because he was a stranger. The idea of being a stranger to her bothered him.

He didn't know where they were headed in the next five minutes, much less the next five hours, but they would find a way out. It bothered him that in a matter of days or weeks she'd forget this interlude. He found it suddenly unacceptable that if she thought about him at all after this was over, she would remember him as a stranger.

For a man who'd constructed his life on the basis of having no permanent ties to anyone outside the job, he knew this was a dangerous mental path.

For a man who, for the first time in his thirty-one years, was beginning to miss having a personal life, it was even scarier.

"My folks died when I was eleven. After that I was raised by my grandparents in the Northwest Territories," he said finally. Maybe if he shared something of his past, she'd feel more comfortable. He ignored the truth that he wanted her to know him as well as he wanted to know her. "They ran a sawmill."

She turned toward him, her eyes wide. "Your family are loggers?"

He kept his gaze steadily on her. "Yes. Three generations back. You a tree hugger, Ms. King?"

She laughed. "Oh, I've hugged my share, but not the way you mean. I have a healthy respect for the forest. I understand the need to retain old growth, but I also understand the value of the lumber industry, both economically and environmentally." There was a definite twinkle in her eyes. He was captivated.

"Then why the surprised reaction?"

He could swear her cheeks pinkened. Must be the sun putting some color back in her skin. No way could he make Jenna King blush. But the idea provoked his imagination further.

"It was just, after my Paul Bunyan cracks, I thought it was too funny that—" She turned back to the baby, shaking her head once again. "Why don't I just swallow my foot once and for all," she said disgustedly. She looked back to him. "I'm sorry. More now than before. I know what it's like being the subject of ridicule, and there is no excuse for doing it to someone else."

"It's really okay, Jenna." He waited, and she finally looked back at him. "Paul Bunyan comparisons were the least of my problems growing up. And I did grow *up*."

Jenna giggled, then stopped, seeming almost embarrassed by the outburst. "I wish I could be as blasé and good-natured about it as you are. Being five-foot-eleven by age fourteen was a nightmare for me."

"I imagine it's a whole different ball game for a woman. I'm sorry it was tough for you. A shame we didn't go to the same school. I'd have protected you."

She smiled at him, but her eyes were tinged with remembered pain. "Oh, I didn't need protecting."

"Big brother?"

Deeper pain flashed across her face, but this time she didn't look away. "No, my brother died when I was fifteen. I was the oldest, and I'd learned long before that to fight my own battles."

"My turn to be sorry. I didn't have any brothers or sisters. I've lost other friends over the years, but losing family is something you never truly get over."

She looked down, but he saw her pull in a deep breath and release it on a long, soft exhale. "Yeah," she said quietly.

"Never leaves you altogether," he said. "I was in my second year with the army when I got word that my grandfather died. Heart attack. By the time I arranged leave to go home, I got word that my grandmother had passed in her sleep. She'd been sick for some time, so that wasn't a real shock. But both of them being gone so suddenly like that . . ." He closed his eyes for a second, then looked up at the now blazing blue sky. "I stayed awhile after the funerals to take care of all the personal stuff and make arrangements to sell the mill to Pap's foreman. His family had been in logging every bit as long as mine had. It was all arranged, they'd both been really smart about setting things up for when they were gone. Still . . . it hit me really hard then how all alone I truly was. Almost worse than when I was a kid. I'd always been independent, not really a loner, not by choice anyway. I never doubted my ability to take care of myself. Far from it. I guess that's why it surprised me at how hard it was to adjust. I don't know—" He broke off and laughed a bit self-consciously. "Gee, this is an uplifting topic."

"I understand better than you might think." Her expression remained somber. "What did you do? After the army, I mean. I take it you hadn't planned to go into the family business either."

"I still work for Uncle Sam," he said, clamping down his jaw a bit as the throb in his knee deepened.

Talking was a tried-and-true method for directing his focus away from his pain. Talking to Jenna, listening to her, soothed something far deeper.

A small smile curved her mouth. "The army is getting lax on haircuts."

"I'm not army any longer. I got out about ten years ago."

Her smile grew. "Oh, that's right, now you rescue people. What branch is that again?"

"Very funny. Actually, if my current boss found out about my little detour today, I'd never live it down."

"Is that where you were headed today? On your flight, I mean. Back to work?"

One simple question, and it hit him like a ton of bricks. *He didn't want to go back.* Several moments passed as the shock of that truth and all its implications began to sink in. She was staring at him, waiting. "I was going to Denver," he said absently. Not go back? Ridiculous. Where in the hell else did he have to go? He'd just gotten done telling her he had no family. The Dirty Dozen was his family.

And what did that say about him? his mind queried. His family was a team of specially trained agents whose only unifying bond was that they weren't bonded to anyone. But he liked that, he responded silently. He fit in there.

Lying there on his back, looking up at the blue October sky over forests of trees that had graced these Oregon mountains for generations, he suddenly saw his life in an entirely different way.

He had fit in. Recruited by Seve Delgado right out of the army, he'd found his work for the Dirty Dozen to be the challenge he'd always wanted. They had fought long and hard against diminishing odds to complete the next-to-impossible tasks they were given. World-weary, jaded, and cynical were all words that could be used to describe any one of them. All except T.J. For a boy raised in the back of beyond, he'd looked at each Dirty Dozen mission as a new adventure and had tackled each one with exuberance that constantly made him the butt of his teammates' many good-natured jokes.

"You don't sound too upset about it."

He looked over at Jenna. "No. I guess I'm not." Saying it out loud somehow cemented the feeling. Suddenly, crawling all over the globe, risking his hide by pulling people out of impossible situations didn't sound nearly as exciting as lying in the middle of Nowhere, Oregon, next to a llama stuck in the mud and talking to Jenna King.

Maybe it was time for a new kind of adventure.

Jenna watched as a bemused smile crossed his face. She didn't know what to make of this man, this purported rescuer of people. He made her feel emotions she'd long ago determined not to feel. If she were honest, she'd admit he made her *want* to feel them. But she was weary of emotional honesty. Having been dragged repeatedly through that dangerous and painful minefield these last several months, she didn't trust anything right now, especially her emotions.

No more personal chitchat. She had enough on her plate. There was no room for T.J., no matter how delectable a side dish he might have turned out to be. The food analogy made her stomach grumble, reminding her of another problem they would soon face.

She didn't care if he flew to Denver or the moon when they got out of there, she told herself, she just wanted out.

A sigh of frustrated resignation slipped through her lips as she resolutely turned back to the baby. "First we have to get you free."

The oozing muck was thickening fairly quickly now as the sun continued to rise and shine. She scooted a bit and reached over, snagging her mud-crusted crutch.

"What's your plan?" he asked.

To get out of here so I can begin figuring out what I'm going to do with my life. And so I can begin forgetting you. She shut out the voices in her head, especially the soft ones whispering that forgetting T. J. Delahaye was not going to be the simpler of those two tasks.

"The mud is getting firmer," she said. "I think I can dig her feet out now. She should be able to get up then."

"Make sure you clear out of the way of those feet. The soles are padded, but the toenails can get you."

She turned. "Toenails? You mean hooves?"

"No. I mean toenails. Two on each foot."

"Where did you learn about llamas? Not in Canada."

"Nope. The Andes Mountains. Peru."

Don't ask, she schooled herself. *You don't want to know.* Oh, but she did. *You don't need to know.* She glanced back at him, his big, gloriously half-naked body all stretched out, a friendly smile on his face.

"I was there for twelve weeks," he went on, taking the decision from her hands. She supposed she could have told him to shut up, but that would be rude.

"The terrain we had to work with wasn't the greatest, but these guys"—he dipped his chin, indicating the baby—"go just about anywhere. They don't pack out with much weight, but they never lose their footing, and they're more reliable than mules or donkeys. They also have a three-part stomach, which is incredibly fuel-efficient, so they don't eat as much either."

"A regular *Wild Kingdom* of llama knowledge."

"Hey, it was cold and lonely up there. You get to know your llama."

His grin was irrepressible, and she found herself returning it. "I'll bet."

"You should be thankful. If I hadn't understood the signs and warned you, that llama spit would have landed—"

She raised her hand. "Yes, yes. Thank you ever so much." She remembered him calming the baby down earlier. What was it he had called her? "What does *cria* mean?"

"Baby llama. In Spanish."

It was on the tip of her tongue to ask him if he spoke Spanish or any other language fluently and exactly what sort of job had taken him to the mountains of Peru and had he been successful and— She was chitchatting again.

You're doing more than that, Jenna. You like this man. He likes you.

She abruptly turned back to the baby and began talking to her softly as she resumed the chore at hand, carefully wedging her crutch into the thicker mud and scooping chunks away, flinging them toward the drier land opposite the streambed.

About fifteen minutes later she'd freed one foot and most of another. The baby had struggled several times, but she'd managed to calm her down each time by stroking her side or neck and talking quietly. T.J. had remained, thankfully, silent. Unfortunately, her rebellious inner voices hadn't. She was exhausted, both mentally and physically, and didn't know how much longer she could keep up the fight.

Halfway through unearthing the third foot, the baby decided she was through waiting and made a determined effort to get up.

"Look out!" T.J. called.

Jenna swung away as the baby began its awkward lunge upward, then scooted back as quickly as she could as the llama struggled to an uneven stand.

"She's huge," Jenna said, staring up at the beast.

"Fit's right in here, then, doesn't she?"

Jenna snapped her gaze to his guileless teasing one, but somehow couldn't take offense. After all, he was including himself in the joke.

As if he could read her mind, he said, "Amazing

how sharing a joke instead of being the butt of one can change your perspective, isn't it?"

She nodded, feeling her fragile wall of resistance to him fracturing once again. He understood her. Too well.

The llama finally extracted herself completely from the mud and, after a moment spent getting her bearings, wandered toward T.J.

"Maybe we should call her Babe," T.J. suggested, lifting a hand from his supine position so the baby could sniff him. "You know, complete the Bunyan connection. I mean, she's not blue, but she's—"

"Not a babe either," Jenna said, covering her mouth on a snort of laughter.

T.J. looked from her to the llama to her and back again. "Hey now, she may not be beautiful at the moment all mud-caked but—" Then his eyes widened and he laughed. "Oh," he said, staring at the underbelly of the beast. "I see what you mean. Okay, so maybe Bob would be a more appropriate name."

His gaze caught Jenna's, and they both laughed. The connection felt good and warm and right and— she abruptly turned away, pulled in a long, steadying breath, and scooped up her crutch. "Whatever his name is, he's free now and looks okay to me. We'd better stop wasting time and figure out how the hell we're going to get out of here."

SEVEN

"I studied a map of the area before I, uh . . . this morning. The main road is up there on the other side of the ridge." She pointed back toward the trees in the direction of the trail they'd both begun the day on. "The only other thing around are back roads, but some lead to private properties. If we can get to one of those, we can—"

"Why did you leave Paradise Canyon, Jenna?" His quiet question brought an immediate halt to her nervous chatter. She was afraid. Of him, of her predicament, he wasn't sure. Maybe both. But she was more afraid of talking about it than anything else. Every time he got close, she pulled back faster and blustered stronger. He wasn't fooled. And he was done backing off.

He didn't know what Jenna wanted, but what she needed was a friend. She needed someone who was willing to brave all her fierce arm-distancing tactics and get to the real woman underneath. He could be that friend.

He watched as the color that had drained from her face at his question slowly seeped back in, as if she'd willed it back. She was one tough lady. He admired her guts and tenacity. He also respected her fear and didn't want to hurt her.

"It was time to go," she said, her expression as implacable as her tone.

"I believe they'd have let you take a cab."

Her brown eyes sent him a warning. "I preferred to hike out."

"Is there someone out there somewhere expecting you?"

Her brows pulled together, and he lifted his hand to stall the retort. The baby licked his palm. T.J. rubbed its muzzle but kept his gaze squarely on Jenna. "What I meant was, will there be anyone worrying that you haven't shown up? Will anyone be out hunting for you?"

The furrows between her brows smoothed, but she shifted her gaze back to her makeshift crutches, absently knocking off chunks of dried mud. She let the silence spin out another couple of seconds, then quietly said, "No. No one is waiting for me."

T.J. decided it was just as well he was flat out on his back. Because if he'd been able to, he would have gone to her, pulled her into his lap, and rocked her against his chest. He fought a small smile. If he hadn't been flat on his back before, he likely would be if he pulled that "macho maneuver" with her.

He watched her braid swing over her shoulder, the lighter strands that wisped free catching the sunlight and causing sparkles of gold to dance along the twined rope of hair like fairy dust. His arms ached with the need to hold her. He wanted to stroke her, to tie up all her loose ends, to make her smile reach all the way up to her eyes.

As if sensing her melancholy, Bob the llama wandered back over to her and nudged at her head. T.J. smiled when the llama persisted and she finally reached up to stroke his neck and scratch him behind his ears. *Way to go, Bob. Give her comfort whether she wants it or not.* Someone sure as hell needed to. T.J. mentally shook his head. Whoever thought he'd be reduced to allowing a llama to act as a stand-in?

"Well," he said cheerfully, "the good news is that people will be looking for me."

She leaned back, looking past the llama's neck at him, her expression emotionless. "We aren't remotely near the trails from Paradise. I wasn't on a regular trail to begin with. We're proverbial needles in a haystack out here."

"We could be tracked relatively easily. You left a trail of clothes down the mountainside where we fell. It stopped raining soon enough that the mud tracks will make our progress from there easy to follow."

"Are you always so relentlessly optimistic?"

"Yep." He shrugged lightly at her scowl, biting down on the wince as his shoulder protested. What his body wouldn't give for a nice, soft bed right now. He found his gaze wandering the generous length of

Jenna's body. Her softer parts would do as well, he thought with a sigh. Better even. "What have you got to lose by thinking positively?" he asked, wondering if she heard the longing.

"Hope."

It was the total absence in her voice of that very thing that banished his fanciful imaginings and brought his attention abruptly back to her face. She'd ducked her head, apparently wishing she hadn't spoken out loud.

He spoke quietly. "If you always expect the worst, then you never had hope to begin with."

The silence stretched on so long, he thought she wouldn't respond, then she said, "But you're never disappointed either." Her tone was weary, beyond physical exhaustion. She sounded completely wrung out.

Treading carefully but determinedly, he said, "Whatever disappointed you must have been horrible if it's taken away your hope. I think that might be the worst thing you could ever lose."

He waited, but she didn't answer. Her gaze was fixed on some unknown point farther down the narrow valley.

"Did it have something to do with why you were at Paradise Canyon? Or why you took off with all your clothes stuffed in a laundry bag?" He waited. Still nothing. "I'll tell you my story, if you tell me yours." Light teasing didn't provoke any reaction, positive or negative. Hell, but the woman was more self-contained than the hardest Dirty Dozen agent.

He'd spent his entire career respecting his team-mates' needs for privacy and had never pushed those boundaries, as they were the foundation that allowed the team to function.

Somehow he couldn't do that with Jenna King. He couldn't even consider it. She needed him. He couldn't explain or analyze why he was so convinced of this, but he knew it to be a hard, fast truth.

Ten years of working with ultra-private colleagues had also taught him a thing or two about how to deal with stubborn, reclusive, self-reliant types. He might not have pushed the boundaries . . . but that didn't mean he hadn't learned how to go around them when necessary.

Different people required different tactics. But this time he decided to follow an adage that had held true throughout most of his career. If the stubborn, reclusive, self-reliant mountain wouldn't come to him . . . He steeled himself for the strong rebuttal his leg was certain to deliver when he asked it to move. He wasn't disappointed. He clenched his jaw hard as he moved to his good side, a grunt slipping out as he levered to a sitting position. Bob and Jenna both turned. He wasn't sure, but he thought they both frowned.

"What are you doing?" Jenna asked.

"Trying to get you to talk to me."

"Well, I'm not that great a conversationalist. Certainly not worth hurting yourself worse over. Lie down before you fall down."

T.J. smiled. "Aw, and here I didn't think you cared."

"I don't." Her narrowed eyes challenged him to say otherwise.

He shrugged and winced, but remained sitting upright. He looked to Bob. "She's crazy about me, really."

Bob made a small snort.

Her eyes widened. "I'm stuck in the middle of nowhere with Jack the Wounded Giant and Bob the Spitting Llama, who are having a conversation while I'm the only one who seems the least bit worried about getting out of here. Which one of us is crazy?"

"The *J* stands for Jefferson."

Her mouth opened, then closed again as she looked at him, confused. "What are you talking—Jefferson?"

He nodded. "Not Jack."

She paused. "Oh please, don't tell me. The *T* isn't for—"

"Thomas."

She dipped her chin. He thought she might have been holding back a smile. "Your mother named you Thomas Jefferson?"

He shook his head. "My dad. His family had a thing for politics. Goes way back. Granddad got off real lucky. His name is Andrew Jackson. Folks called him A.J. T.J. was sort of a natural nickname, considering. My father wasn't as lucky. He was Woodrow Wilson Delahaye. Everyone called him Woody. You can imagine the lumber jokes he put up with." He thought her eyes were starting to tear up from the effort of suppressing laughter. Of course, they could also be glazing over from boredom. He grinned. "It could have been a lot worse for me. I could have been Abe, Calvin, Herbert. . . ." He thought for a moment and made a face. "Or Dwight."

Jenna slid her hand over her mouth, but not in time to stop the giggle that burst out. "I'm sorry," she said on a restoring breath. "Really I am. It's just . . ."

"Rutherford."

Another snort escaped her, then another.

"Ulysses."

That put her over, and she gave in to it and laughed out loud, finally holding her side with one hand and wiping her eyes with the other.

"I bet you have no idea how stunning you are when you smile like that. You have a wonderful laugh."

She sobered instantly.

He smiled a bit sadly, but he wasn't sorry for the compliment. She would damn well have to get used to them. "I'm not teasing you. Why do you shut down like that? In fact, I've never been so sincere. You're a stunning woman. Surely people have complimented you before?"

It was her turn to shrug. Bob had wandered downstream and found some grass to munch on. She turned to watch him.

T.J. frowned. "I'm not trying to make you uncomfortable."

"Well, you've failed another mission," she said, her back still to him. She poked the end of her crutch into the soft mud, drawing lines then watching the mud ooze back in and erase the crease.

T.J. watched her for several silent moments. Her arms were long and well toned, her hands big and able. Her extended legs were long, her thighs well developed through the snug fit of her damp jeans. Her muddy sock-clad foot, even swollen, was not a dainty size. No, for all her height, she was no waif-thin-model type. Far from it.

To him she was gorgeous. Every big, strong, lean inch of her. But there was a delicacy to her too. It was there in the long bones of her fingers and the graceful line of her neck. He remembered the velvet-soft brush of her eyelashes and the soft curve of her cheek. Add to that the shadows of vulnerability, that almost glass-thin fragility that occasionally haunted her eyes, and the fierce way she protected anyone from seeing it. She was an anomaly, an intriguing mixture of emotions. Watching her was like staring through a kaleidoscope, entranced by the never-ending patterns created at each tumble of the multicolored bits of glass. She captivated him, totally and completely. He found it impossible to believe he was the only one to find her so.

As she continued to poke at the mud he continued to poke at her, tumbling those pieces, wondering what pattern he'd find this time. "I apologize for making you feel awkward. But not for the compliment."

"Apology accepted."

"What about the compliment."

She huffed a sigh of frustration and turned to him. "Okay, okay, thank you already. Now can we talk about getting us out of here?"

T.J.'s grin was wolfish. "Your eyes are beautiful when you yell at me." She glared at him. He winked at her.

Jenna threw her crutch down, startling Bob, who swung his head up and stared balefully at her. She growled. "You're insufferable. Has anybody ever told you that?"

"Almost daily."

"Did it ever occur to you, it wasn't a compliment?"

"Nope. Never even crossed my mind." T.J. looked away, his attention reluctantly caught by Bob. "He's wandering farther away." He sighed to himself. *Just when I was getting somewhere.*

Jenna turned and looked too. The baby was almost fifty yards away and ambling farther downstream. "At least he's smart enough to try and save himself." She didn't voice her apprehension over letting the baby wander off on his own.

"Maybe he can save us too."

She looked at T.J. "He's a baby. And even if he wasn't, I don't think you can ride a llama."

"I didn't mean that."

Jenna looked back toward Bob. "We can't go after him." It wasn't until she turned back and caught the look of compassion on T.J.'s face that she realized she'd revealed her feelings anyway. She straightened and picked up her crutches. "He was on his own before and seemed to be okay. I mean, he's ugly and he spits, but he didn't look starved or anything. He'll be fine on his own."

"I never suggested he wouldn't be," T.J. said softly.

It was his gentle, understanding tone that snapped it. "You suggested he was going to save us, and I'm trying to point out that the only one he's saving is himself. I don't care what he does or where he goes."

"Liar," he said easily.

She ground her teeth. "Will you stop it?"

"Stop what?"

She flung her hand toward him, gesturing at his face. "That!" she said. "That way you look at me all patient and understanding. It drives me crazy."

"I can see that. It's not my intention."

His continued calm riled her further. "Don't you ever lose your temper? Doesn't anything get to you? And what's with the questions? You're treating me like a . . . like a . . ."

"Friend?"

That made her pause, but only for a second. Her hold on everything was far too tenuous to give in to the temptation of contemplating how an offer of friendship from T.J. Delahaye made her feel. "I don't need a friend. What I need is a helicopter or a horse or some damn way to get off this godforsaken mountain."

"What you need is a friend who won't give up on

you even when you try to bully them into leaving. Why is it so hard to admit you need help? It doesn't diminish your strength, Jenna. I can't imagine anyone would question your competence at anything you choose to do because you ask for assistance."

His statement took her so off guard, she had to stop and think it over to make sure she'd heard him correctly. Unfortunately, she had. The very idea that he'd come to understand her so well despite her attempts to keep him at arm's length terrified her. She didn't want to be probed or examined anymore. Not even by this man who could make her laugh and swear and laugh again, all in the space of five minutes. Especially not by him.

"What I need is for you to back off with this pop-psychology crap and let me figure out a way to get us out of here before nightfall. We might be having unseasonably warm days, but this late in October the nights can be brutally cold at this elevation."

"Am I such a bad deal?" he said, ignoring her dire warning. "I mean, I know my rescue attempt left me a bit less than a hundred percent, but at least I'm a decent guy. You could have been trapped out here with an ax murderer."

"At least an ax murderer would have either put me out of my misery or provided a functional tool I could use."

He grinned. "Sorry, I wasn't planning to rescue damsels today. Babe the Blue Ox and I usually reserve that for alternate Tuesdays."

She threw up her hands. "This is ridiculous. You

are ridiculous, not to mention crazy. How do you pull me into these senseless conversations?"

"Practice?" he suggested. "Hey," he said, unperturbed by her fierce glower, "I was trying to get your mind off your problems. You worry too much."

She grabbed at her other crutch and struggled painfully to her feet. Her hands hurt like hell. The ground-in mud and silt wasn't helping matters. She clamped her teeth together as she tried to corral her temper. The wave of pain from her ankle as she wobbled fully upright made her slightly nauseous. She waited a second for it to pass before she looked at him.

Her fury banked, at least temporarily, she spoke with as much quiet dignity as she could muster—and given how she'd yelled like a banshee, and probably looked like one, too, her reserves of dignity were definitely running low.

"You don't know me, and you don't have any idea what I've been through or what is worth worrying about in my life. I know you think you're helping me, but you're not. Please, leave it alone." *Leave me alone*. T.J. made her feel at a time when numbness was a merciful relief.

"I wasn't making idle conversation, Jenna. I've spent most of my life keeping to myself and respecting the space of others. My job demands it. My motives here aren't self-serving. I look at you and see a desirable, intelligent woman who, under any circumstances, I'd be interested in knowing. If that was all there was to it, and you made it clear the interest was not reciprocal, I'd slink off and lick my wounds in private. As I said, my life is solitary by choice, and I long ago stopped wishing I could have it both ways."

She found herself turning to look at him.

"But I look at you and I also see someone who is hurting. Deeply. And I'm finding it impossible to sit by and watch you suffer. So, again, I'll apologize for making you uncomfortable, I sincerely don't want to add to your pain. But I also think that interest isn't entirely unreciprocated . . . and that makes me push a bit harder."

"Maybe I don't like being pushed."

"And maybe you're not used to someone who'll push harder than you."

There wasn't a trace of the gentle, teasing man left. In front of her now was a man she'd only glimpsed, the serious determined man who'd ordered her to prop up her foot or else. She'd learned early on that one benefit to her height was the ability it gave her to control most situations. It was a weapon she'd often exploited.

Where ego and confidence in men was concerned, she'd dealt with the elite corps of the species and had won the battle handily. She didn't like having to admit that she was intimidated by T.J., by the intensity of his interest in her. Most men shrugged and walked away after a few well-aimed barbs, leaving her safely believing they weren't really interested anyway. At least that's what she'd always told herself. It wasn't until now, with T.J., that Jenna was forced to wonder if her defensive tactics weren't protection at all, but some sort of test. A test she specifically set men up to fail. That way it was their fault, not hers—after all, they'd proven they weren't worth the risk of putting her emotions and heart on the line.

So where did that put Delahaye relative to other men?

Nothing daunted him. She swallowed hard as a small shiver of pleasure buzzed along her spine, as unnerving as it was tantalizing. He teased her with personal information as he badgered her for the same, and it galled her to admit his strategy was working. Despite all her internal warnings, she was still revealing things about herself she hadn't intended to— and dying to find out more about him.

She looked down at her hands and tightened her grip on her crutches until her knuckles turned white. The stabbing pain didn't help her focus this time. Delahaye would not be controlled either by her size or her temper. She was defenseless against him. "I don't want to talk about it."

"Maybe you should. Maybe it will help."

Fear made her temper flame hotter. "And maybe it's none of your damn business."

"I'm trying to be your friend, Jenna."

"You tried to rescue me, too, and see where that got me?"

"Are you this hard on everyone, or is it just me? Don't you ever let anyone close?"

"Not if I can help it. Not anymore, anyway."

His eyes sparked with interest. She immediately

realized her mistake. Couldn't she simply shut up around this man?

"Jenna—"

"I think our energy is better spent on finding a way out of here," she said abruptly, and not for the first time. Not waiting for a response, she turned and began to make her way slowly downstream, taking the same route as the baby—who was no longer in sight.

"Can I ask where you're going?"

His dry sarcasm was something of a relief. He was going to stop his probing. Thank God, she thought fervently. Her old defenses didn't work against him, and he wasn't giving her the chance to develop new ones. She needed time. And distance.

She didn't turn around but continued her careful progress, whistling on a pained breath each time she leaned her weight into the crutches. "After the llama," she ground out. "Maybe the ranch he came from isn't too far from here. If it hasn't burned to the ground, there might be help. We might at least find shelter or food."

"Gee, why didn't I think of that?"

Maybe the llama can save us. Heat warmed her cheeks, but she pressed on. She was getting used to the taste of her own foot in her mouth, but she was through apologizing to him. "Don't worry, I won't abandon you. If I don't see anything soon, I'll come back and we'll figure out something else for tonight." She resolutely refused to think about the fact that the only source of heat that would be available to them was body heat.

The memory of waking up in his big warm embrace flooded her mind anyway. Time and what had passed between them since that moment hadn't diminished in the least the wondrous sensation of being cared for. She ruthlessly shoved it away.

"You can't take any hills, up or down, on that ankle, even with those crutches."

She wasn't all too sure she could handle another ten feet of relatively flat ground, but she'd die before she admitted it. She pressed on. "Bob isn't going to wait around, so I have to try."

She covered another ten or so yards before she allowed herself to believe he would let her escape in peace. As much as it stung her pride, she knew damn well her pursuit of Bob was not entirely motivated by their need for help. She also knew there was little doubt that T.J. understood this too.

A loud grunt followed by a string of curse words that even her fellow jumpers would have been impressed with shattered her final illusion. There would never be peace in her life as long as T. J. Delahaye was around.

She looked back to see him slowly climbing to a stand. He was relying heavily on his crutches. It hurt to watch him.

"What in the blazes do you think you're doing?" she demanded, though she knew the answer with dreaded certainty.

"Coming with you."

"But . . . but . . . you can't!" She was sputtering and quickly worked at smoothing her tone. "You'll slow me down," she said sharply.

"Yeah, you're cruising along at warp speed here."

"My point exactly," she said. "I'm already hobbling. Unless Bob is sampling creek grass along the way, I probably won't catch up as it is. I can't wait around for you."

"I don't recall asking you to," he said, the subtle chide effective despite the strain in his voice. "But I'm not waiting for you to come back either."

She turned to face him. The pain in her ankle pulsed stronger and hotter as her blood pressure—and fear—soared. "What, because I don't want to open a vein and bleed my personal life history all over you, you think I'd leave you out here?"

For a huge man with one knee in a makeshift brace, he was disgustingly graceful—and surprisingly swift. He closed the remaining distance between them, his face set in a mask of implacable determination. She wanted to back away but didn't. Couldn't.

Even hunched on his crutches as he was, she had to look up to hold his gaze. A host of new sensations rushed through her. He made her feel small, vulnerable. Feminine.

When he spoke again his voice was a dark, pain-laced murmur. "No, Jenna King, I don't think you'd ever abandon a responsibility, no matter how much you resent being saddled with it."

His perceptiveness on top of his raw sensuality shook her badly. She was both overwhelmed by and woefully unprepared for the feelings he was arousing in her. His voice, deep and strained, still stroked her like black velvet. And if his voice hadn't trapped her, the steel in his eyes would have. They were as hard as his voice was soft, forbidding her to look away, forcing her to hear his words and deal with them . . . forcing her to deal with him.

She was helpless against this, having no idea how to combat the force of nature that was T.J. Delahaye. *Why combat it?* her little voice asked. *Why not give in, explore it? Explore what he makes you feel?*

She shook her head, as if the action would negate the thoughts. "If you trust me to help you," she said, forcing the words out on a less than steady breath, "then why are you following me?"

A wicked grin slowly transformed his serious expression into one that could only be described as . . . predatory. What little hope she had left of regaining control of the situation fled in a rush of pure primal panic.

He leaned in a little closer. "Maybe I don't want to be a loner anymore."

EIGHT

T.J. watched, mesmerized by the way black pupils absorbed rich brown irises, heating up her eyes. Tendrils of dark blond hair clung to her forehead and cheekbones. Desire pulsed, fierce and deep within him. She looked wild, untamed. He felt . . . primitive.

He had to taste her or go crazy. He lowered his mouth, knowing he had long since passed that point, then delighted in the discovery that he had to do little more than dip his head to reach her lips.

Her lips. Were they as soft as they were sassy? A groan built in his throat as his body tightened further. Pain from his various injuries took a backseat to a more immediate, demanding ache.

He heard the soft intake of breath as her lips parted, but answered to the pull of her gaze, feeling the intensity even as he lifted his eyes to hers. They were wide with fear, of what he wasn't exactly sure.

But they were also dark with want and need. He didn't stop.

"What do you taste like, Jenna King?" Her eyes widened further at his rough whisper. He dropped his gaze to her mouth, felt another hard punch of desire, then let his eyes drift shut as he claimed her.

Sweet with a little spice. Exactly how she should taste, he thought, sinking deeper into the kiss even as he worked to keep his response under control. Their only contact was their lips; not being able to touch her with his hands was both frustrating and erotic.

"Open for me," he said against her lips. There were other avenues he could explore.

"T.J." His name had never sounded so wonderful.

He wanted to take her fast and hard, but hearing her speak was almost as tantalizing, so he forced himself to pull back. He teased her with small kisses to the corner of her mouth, gently tugging at the fullness of her lower lip as he worked his way to the other side.

She hadn't moved away or in any way tried to end their singular connection, but she hadn't joined in as an active participant either. He wanted badly to change that. "Kiss me, Jenna."

She withdrew, only slightly, but he cursed silently. He should have known better, he should have taken her with him for the ride. But while that would have been mutually enjoyable, it wouldn't have been entirely satisfying. For either of them.

Her breathing was rapid and a bit shallow. "T.J., I . . ." She averted her gaze and tucked her chin.

His lips brushed against her forehead. "It's just a kiss." He would have given anything to be able to touch her at that moment, to stroke her cheek, lift her chin, bring her gaze back to his. He was leaning too heavily on his makeshift crutches to chance it. It was costing him to stay upright. They'd likely end up in a heap in the muck. "Jenna, look at me."

He waited patiently, doubting she'd allow herself to hide for long. She waited long enough to make him wonder, but finally lifted her head. Her eyes were still dark with desire but also troubled. Not with fear exactly, he thought, tumbling headlong into their depths, but certainly they were filled with doubts. He wasn't sure how to allay those doubts, or why it was so important that he do so. He pushed on, working on instinct. He'd analyze his mistakes later.

"What are you afraid of?" The instant the words were out he wanted to kick himself. *Way to go, Delahaye. What instincts are you working with anyway? Suicidal ones?*

He opened his mouth to retract the question—he should have gone ahead and kissed her—but she surprised him and spoke.

"I'm afraid that . . ." She trailed off, shifting her gaze somewhere past his shoulder, but he schooled himself to patience. No more pushing. Not yet anyway. She must have sensed his unspoken decision. He watched, his smile one of affection, as she gathered her control. It was nothing obvious, a slight stiffening of her spine, a straighter line across her shoulders, a hint of a lift to her chin when she looked back at him.

He released a short breath he hadn't been aware of holding. Desire, concern, doubts, they were all still there in her eyes. Only now they were tempered with determination. On some deeper level he knew that had been no small accomplishment for her. He wanted to cheer.

He wanted to kiss her.

"I'm afraid that . . ." she began again, her voice steadier but still nerve-revvingly raspy. He loved her deep throaty voice. It made him think of dark whispers shared between damp cotton sheets, the air all humid with the heat generated from two sweat-slicked bodies sliding over and into each other. Her back stiffened further, and she held his gaze more directly, the familiar bluff of arrogance returning. He wondered what she might have seen in his eyes. He'd been too busy spinning fantasies to worry about concealing his thoughts.

"I'm afraid that, as obnoxious and inept as you may be, that I'll . . . that I might like it." Her lips twitched, but the fine tremor in her jaw told him it was nerves, not suppressed laughter.

The idea that she might—*might!*—like his kisses terrified her!

Erotic fantasies fled. T.J. was stunned. He may have committed himself to a job requiring a solitary lifestyle, but he'd had his share of relationships. Brief though they may have been, he'd encountered fear of commitment, fear of lack of commitment, fear of pain, either emotional or physical, but fear of pleasure? He had no idea how to deal with her.

He adopted a cocky grin, though this time he felt anything but. "If you don't enjoy it, then I'm not doing something right." Her expression didn't change. He grew serious. "I don't want to hurt you." He watched her carefully for signs he was headed in the right direction. Later he'd question why it was so critical that he not make a misstep with her. "But someone else already has, right?"

"Several somebodies." There was no tentativeness in her voice now. Her words were as cold and hard as steel, as if she were daring him to make something of it.

Her frankness touched him. And surprised him. She may be full of bold bluster and overt confidence, but he knew that was her way of shielding the truth— the truth that she was as vulnerable and insecure as the next person, perhaps more so. That she'd trusted him with that revelation, no matter how belligerently confided, was almost as good as a kiss. Almost.

His grin returned to play at the corners of his mouth. "Well, with someone as obnoxious and inept as me, what have you really got to lose?"

Her lips twitched again, this time with humor. "It's already cost you an arm and a leg. Do you really want to risk more?"

His mind automatically inserted "my heart." It had taken a surprising measure of control not to speak it out loud. *His heart?* It wasn't his to give. At least that's what he'd always told himself. He'd long ago dedicated his heart to serving his team, to serving his country. He'd never even questioned it before. It was simply his life. A subject not up for discussion.

Until now. All the questions he'd tried so hard not to ask since coming to Paradise Canyon bubbled and churned inside him again. Questions about his life, his future, his past. Why had coming back to Oregon felt so much like coming home? His family was long gone.

He focused on Jenna, whose faded smile told him his smile had disappeared too. Was that the source of this attraction? Was he testing himself? Was he exploring what he felt with Jenna as a way to prove to himself that he really belonged on that plane, winging his way back to Scottie and the rest of his Dirty Dozen teammates?

Or was he looking for a reason to get out?

Team members couldn't form outside attachments. If he had someone he cared for, loved, he was rendered too vulnerable for the team and thereby ineffective. Was that what he was doing here? Forming an attachment as a way out of the team?

The possibility left him feeling slightly queasy and more than a little out of control. Not even as a child, when his parents had died and his world had spun into a new orbit, had he felt so helpless.

"T.J.?"

Was he using her? He didn't think so. A person couldn't fake this kind of gut reaction. But could his inner turmoil manifest itself this way? Jenna was obviously dealing with some serious issues of her own.

Did he dare continue to explore his feelings if it might hurt her?

Did he dare not?

He forced his mouth to curve as he looked deeply into her eyes. The resulting jump of desire he saw there chose his path for him, the unconscious way she wet her lips shoved him forward. "You know, kissing doesn't have to be serious business, Jenna." He shifted a bit closer, liking the warm feel of her breath on his lips. "It can be for fun." A little closer. "When was the last time you let yourself have fun?" His lips barely brushed hers. "Come on, Jenna. Come play with me."

Playing, that's all this was. *Liar.* T.J. ignored the inner voice and kissed her, keeping the pressure light and gentle, but still coaxing her, urging her to respond. And then he felt it. The subtle pliancy in her lips, the slight tilt of her mouth as she pressed back. His desire for her had been a slow-burning fire. Her sweet response instantly fueled it into a raging inferno, robbing him of oxygen, smothering his control. He wanted to tilt his head back and howl in primal triumph. He wanted to pull her down to the ground and make hot, hungry love to her.

He opened his eyes as she deepened her kiss, and felt his heart squeeze as he saw the soft brush of her eyelashes against her cheek. He schooled himself to patience, slow and steady. Though his body demanded otherwise, this wasn't a race. As badly as he wanted her, he wanted her to enjoy it more.

Then she parted her lips. At the first tentative

touch of her tongue, he groaned and lost what control he'd had. He couldn't pull her into his arms, couldn't ease the insistent ache of his body by grinding it tightly into hers, so he took what he could with what he had. He slanted his mouth across hers, kissing her more fully, demanding a response, becoming even more aroused with the knowledge that the only thing holding her to him was his mouth—and her own need.

She was strong and sexy and oh, so unbearably sweet, it was all he could do not to devour her. He'd never felt such an aching emptiness, a yawning chasm of need that threatened to swallow him up if he didn't fill it.

His doubts about his motivation were shoved ruthlessly to the background as her tongue ran along the surface of his lips. His humming response quickly turned to a growl as he opened his mouth and welcomed her inside. Any fears that she might withdraw vanished as she followed him willingly, tasting him, taking him, dueling with his tongue as if the intimate dance between them had been choreographed long ago.

He had to touch her, had to feel her skin under his palms, had to hold her, mold her strength and perfect length to his, and he had to do it now or go stark raving mad. Hell, he was already there. Never had he felt such desires—to take and protect, to consume and be consumed—licking at his control, teasing his mind, taunting his heart.

Without conscious thought he had begun to shift

his weight to his good leg when a loud whining bleat cut through the air, surprising them apart.

"Bob," they said simultaneously on unsteady breaths.

"He's hurt himself," Jenna said, worry and disgust in her voice.

T.J. would have been amused by that oh-so-Jenna combination if he hadn't been so disgusted . . . and disappointed himself. "He better be dangling from a cliff by his two-toed feet, or I'm having llamaburgers for dinner."

Jenna's eyes widened with offense, but her mouth curved in a dry smile. "Yeah, he'd better be in pain, or he's llama meat. That makes perfect sense, Delahaye."

T.J. grumbled, but his lips were twitching. "I didn't want to be interrupted. If I have to be in pain, then, well . . ." He lifted one shoulder in a shrug. "Sue me."

"Your leg. T.J., I told you to lie down, instead of . . . of . . ."

"Oh, I was more than willing to lie down, Jenna." He dropped his voice and leaned in close, his breath mingling with hers when he spoke. "And Bob-burgers or no, we're not done yet. Not by a long shot."

Jenna stared at him. Her gaze dropped to his mouth then darted back to his eyes. Suddenly she was all business. "I'd better go find out where he is this time." She hopped back on her crutches, putting a foot or so of space between them. "It doesn't sound like he's gone far."

T.J. didn't miss her clenched jaw as she turned. He wasn't the only one with throbbing body parts. He growled under his breath at the unnecessary reminder. "Be careful," he warned. "I know you care, we both do, but don't hurt yourself unnecessarily, Jenna." His voice was sharp with concern.

"You coming or staying?" was all she said, her back to him as she hobbled slowly toward Bob's insistent bleating.

"I'll get there eventually. Don't worry about me."

"Didn't say I was."

T.J. smiled at that. "Yeah well, just in case."

"What, hell freezes over?" She kept moving.

T.J. continued to smile. "That or you let down your guard enough to admit you do care."

"In your dreams, Delahaye," she called back.

"Oh, you can bet you'll play a significant role in those, Hopalong."

All he heard was a snort. His knee screamed bloody murder when he asked it to move, but move it he did. He smiled even as he swore. He might be confused about a lot of stuff right now, but he was crystal clear on one thing. He wasn't through exploring yet. And until he was, he wasn't going to let Jenna King out of his sight.

Jenna clamped her teeth tighter to keep the moans of pain locked in. She'd survived some extremely tough physical tests during her career, but this one ranked right up there at the top. Her ankle had moved beyond throbbing into a steady hot burning pain. The effort required to keep it lifted off the ground made it feel more like an anvil than a foot. She didn't even want to look at her hands. The socks she'd wound on for protection had long ago become one with her skin. Bob's continued braying provided an aptly dour sound track for her unpleasant thoughts. "Yeah, yeah keep your shaggy, mud-caked fur on," she said between pants of exertion. "I'm coming. Again."

Thinking about the llama didn't make her own pain any easier to ignore, but it did help divert her mind from that kiss.

Okay, so it didn't divert all of her mind. She'd obviously lost a good chunk of it back there with T.J. Had that actually been her voice all breathy and bothered? She felt her skin heat up clear down to her chest. It was a good thing she'd been crutch-dependent, or she'd probably have completely humiliated herself and pressed her body right up against T.J.'s smooth, mile-wide chest.

Lord, even standing there doing nothing but grinning, the man made her feel more female than she'd ever come close to feeling in her entire life. And if that weren't enough to tempt a nun to sin, the man kissed like he'd made it his life's work to learn every possible nuance of a woman's mouth and master them all.

Of course, she realized with a small snarl that felt uncomfortably like jealousy, maybe he had. For all she knew, the man had a woman tucked away behind every pine tree in Oregon. And whatever it was he rescued people from, logic dictated that a fair share of his clients were women. Women who'd be more than willing to show their gratitude any way he wanted it to be shown.

Her heart rate sped up again. Her continued exertion in the face of almost total exhaustion was only part of the cause.

Bob's bleat turned into a series of guttural wails, each more pitiful than the last.

She should be thanking Bob, not cursing him. After all, he'd saved her from making a total fool of herself. So why didn't she feel very fortunate? They might have been joined only at the mouth, but T.J. had easily managed to telegraph his wants and desires. And she knew he'd desired her. Her.

She did smile then. It was a heady thing.

It was a ridiculous thing, her inner voice shot back.

She sighed and paused long enough to redistribute her weight on her palms. The rough stubs that formed the uneven Y of the crutch were wreaking havoc on the skin under her arms and above her ribs as well. *Was it really so ridiculous?* she asked silently, her pain, no matter how intense, unable to divert her mind. What would it have hurt to indulge this one time? she wondered. This one time when the attraction was mutual and nothing was at stake but a few new experiences? Nothing would or could come of this unlikely liaison, so why not wander the path to its natural and quite probable mutually satisfying conclusion?

What in the hell else did she have to look forward to anyway?

She moved on, sucking in air as her palms once again gripped the crutches. She purposely didn't look back to see where he was. He was following her. She knew it without having to check. She could feel him behind her.

A small chuckle that sounded more like a sob escaped her tightly pressed lips as she allowed her mind to follow through on their earlier kiss. Even if Bob hadn't interrupted, where could it have gone?

She pictured them lying on the ground writhing . . . in agony. They were both so banged up, they were lucky to have managed the kiss. "Quit while you're ahead for once," she ground out under her breath.

There was a tricky spot ahead, about fifteen or twenty yards wide, where the banks of the stream had overflowed all the way up to the tree line. Even though the water had receded, the mud and muck it left behind provided a serious challenge. One she wasn't sure she was up to. But going around meant going up, and that was definitely not happening.

She traced Bob's path. His two-toed tracks were clear in the mud; deep, but not oozed over. If she was really careful . . .

Jenna mercifully stopped thinking about T.J. and his kisses and focused on navigating herself through the next several yards of mud.

The jagged ends of the crutches spiked into the mud, making forward motion slow and dangerously uneven. Her booted foot sank to the ankle before finding solid ground, forcing her to press harder on her palms in order to pull it out to move forward, only to sink it in again. Each inch forward felt like a mile, but she didn't dare pause, fearing her foot would sink so deeply, she'd get stuck. Again. It was the one thing that kept her pushing on.

Bob's racket was getting louder, which meant she was closer. If she hadn't needed all her breath and then some, she'd have called out to him, tried to soothe him. It was hard to see past the bend, but he had to be past the curve. A few more yards . . .

Jenna groaned. Might as well be a hundred, she thought dispiritedly. As she neared the other side the ground grew firmer. It should have been a relief, but she was so exhausted now, she wasn't sure she could keep herself from collapsing the instant she was on dry, hard land.

"You're almost there, Jenna." The shout surprised her, momentarily making her dip precariously to the right and almost lose her balance. "You can do it."

T.J.'s deep voice was like a stroke of velvet across nerves stretched well past their snapping point. She couldn't turn even her head at this point, her energy focused one hundred percent on the dry patch of dirt and grass less than five feet ahead, but some still-functioning part of her brain guessed he'd begun crossing the mudflats.

His words bolstered her flagging determination

right when she needed it most. She groaned long and loud, past worrying about appearances and pride, as she pulled her foot from the last inch or two of muck and stumbled awkwardly onto solid ground. She'd done it!

Bob chose that moment to let out a particularly sharp-pitched wail. A stark reminder that her mission wasn't over yet. She wanted to lie down and sob. And sleep. She had nothing left. Bob would have to wait until she'd had some rest. A month should do it.

Jenna's gaze was still locked on the soft patch of grass, which by now had assumed oasislike proportions. Her knee was already bending, her mind already halfway to sleep when a panicked series of bleats filled the air.

Through the haze of her exhaustion it occurred to her that the baby llama could probably see her now, and that this was the cause of his excited ruckus. "I'm sorry, Bob," she said, the words more rasp than her intended shout. She tore her gaze from her oasis to look for him. "You're going to have to wa—" She broke off as she spied him, the rest of the sentence lost on a long sigh of relief. "Looks like you found your way home after all."

Or almost.

Bob was stuck in a tangle of broken fencing and barbed wire, part of an otherwise solid wooden fence with barbed wire strung along the top that ran in a northwesterly direction as far as she could see. In the distance she could make out the shapes of several outbuildings. Though it was hard to tell their condition or much else from where she was, they were obviously part of a ranch of some kind. And a ranch meant people. People meant help.

Their ordeal was almost over.

Adrenaline raced through her tired body, but it made her feel queasy rather than energized. There was nothing left to rev up. The ranch was less than a quarter mile away by her estimation, but it might as well have been in the next universe. She had to rest. Right there. Right now.

"Jenna!"

T.J. She spared a shred of mental energy to wonder how he'd managed to make it so far; his knee was worse than her ankle.

Even without the fall, she knew she could no longer hack it. She'd known it when she left Paradise, but only now did the reality of it truly hit her. Despair descended over her like a dark, suffocating cloak, adding its weight to her already formidable burden. She was never going back to the Aerial Fire Depot in Missoula. She was never going back to work for the Forest Service.

She was never going to fight another fire.

Dread sent a sick chill over her skin. She weaved unsteadily as her stomach rolled, wondering if she even had the strength to be sick.

Weak. You're weak, Jenna King. *No!* she shouted silently. *I can't be. I'm strong and able.* A sob escaped her lips. *I have to be. It's the only thing I have.*

"Jenna!"

T.J. was coming for her. Rescue. *Rescue me.* For

some reason her overtaxed brain could no longer fathom, that wasn't supposed to make her feel good, wasn't supposed to bring her comfort. But all she could think of was how good his arms felt wrapped around her, how wonderful she'd felt with his mouth hot and demanding on hers, how heady and powerful she'd felt kissing him back and feeling his response. Powerful. Strong. T.J. Why was that wrong? Her thoughts scattered like bits of paper in the wind; too many, flying in too many directions for her to gather. No control. Frustration. Fear. The awful taste of desperation.

Help me! She felt the ground move under her feet and stared at it, trying to make sense out of everything . . . anything. But it was too hard, and she was too tired. So tired.

"Jenna!"

She shook her head and the world spun. Bob's frantic bleating made her mind spin even more. *Hurry, T.J. Ranch. Rescue.* From someplace deep down inside her, she summoned whatever she had left and called out, "Ranch ahead." Then her body decided that was it. Her knee buckled, and she let the crutches fall as she collapsed to the ground.

NINE

T.J.'s heart stopped when he saw her fall. He'd known she was near the end of her rope. He should have never let her go. *Yeah, right.* No one "let" Jenna King do anything. At any other time he'd have smiled, but right now his stomach was halfway up his throat.

"Damn!" He'd have given anything for two good knees right at that moment. After seeing how far she'd sunk in, he'd managed to maneuver uphill with a sideways hop that wouldn't have won him any grace awards but had enabled him to avoid the mud. He was past the mud now, but he still had to maneuver back down the slope, which was a bit steeper at this end. A small stand of trees kept him from seeing any farther downstream than Jenna's crumpled form, but he knew Bob was just past her.

"Damn llama," he said, trying several different angles for his descent but finding none that wouldn't land him at the bottom of the hill in a heap. And he'd already done that one more time than he needed to today. He swore long and hard as he painfully lowered himself to a sitting position, describing in great detail what he'd do to Bob once he got his hands on him.

He knew none of this was Bob's fault, but it made him feel better to vent his anger and frustration, and picturing Jenna trying to hide her amusement behind offended outrage helped some too.

"Llamaburger, llama pot roast, llama pâté. A nice woolly coat."

He shifted so his back was facing downslope, balanced his crutches across his lap and awkwardly propped his braced leg on the shin of his good one. He began inching backward down the slope. His doctors would be able to retire after he paid for the damage he'd done to himself during this escapade.

Retire.

No. Don't even think it. He shut his mind down to one thing. Get to Jenna, that became his mantra. Seemingly hours later, though it was probably about half of one, he hobbled the final few yards to Jenna's crumpled form.

Despite the dirt streaks and paleness of her skin, she looked like a child at rest. A troubled child. Her mouth was tight rather than relaxed and a small furrow creased the skin between her eyebrows. His fingers flexed around the rough bark of his crutches as he recalled the soft feel of her cheek. She was curled on her side, her mud-caked hands folded under her chin. Her chest rose and fell evenly. She was asleep. T.J. breathed a sigh of relief. Still, he wanted to be sure. He began the arduous task once again of lowering his frame to the ground.

Bob's whiny grunts filled the air. T.J. stopped and reluctantly dragged his gaze away.

"It's okay," he called, his tone soothing, "you big clumsy furball." Bob was tangled up pretty good. He didn't see any blood, but the barbs were meshed well into his fur. Without wire cutters or shears, heaven only knew how he was going to get the silly beast loose. At least he wasn't squirming much, worn out most likely. "Yeah, I'm going to save your hairy backside." T.J.'s voice calmed him. "Just stop wiggling those things in deeper, okay?"

But first he had to make sure Jenna was okay, or at least not any worse.

Several grunts and another string of invectives later, he was seated in the grass by her shoulders. He took a pulse check on her neck, then listened to her respiration. The former was a bit slow, and though her breathing was shallow, it was even. He wanted to check her pupils, but he felt fairly certain she was sleeping not passed out, and he didn't want to wake her yet. God knew they both needed about a week's rest, not to mention medical attention that would probably include a hospital stay.

From his seated position, a slight rise in the terrain and the scrub brush blocked his view of the fence. Jenna's shout had been weak, but he'd heard her cry "ranch" and assumed the fence surrounded one. From what he could tell, there, where the valley spread out a bit wider, some of it had escaped the ravages of fire. He hoped that was true for the rest of the ranch as well. He should get up and check it out and see what he could do about Bob. And he would. In a minute.

She needed more rest. He didn't have the heart to wake her up and make her face one last trek. From the angle of the sun, he estimated several good hours of daylight and warmth still remained. Letting her use one for sleep seemed wise. T.J. couldn't keep his hands away, though. He lightly stroked her cheek and smoothed the wild curls wisping around her face. He wondered how all that thick hair would look when it was unbound. His fingers itched to turn thought to deed.

"I'll see those waves of thick hair. And before we part for good, I'll taste you again, Jenna King." He told himself the soft words were to keep Bob calm, but he knew they were for himself too. Slowly, as he continued to stroke his fingertips over Jenna's forehead and hair, the tenseness in her skin smoothed out and her mouth slowly relaxed. Her breathing slowed and deepened, and he realized after a time that his had slowed to match it. Again and again, he stroked her, quietly stunned by his own reaction. How was it that merely touching this woman brought him a peace he couldn't recall ever feeling?

He traced his fingers lightly down her cheek and under her mouth, wanting to continue until he'd memorized the feel of every inch of her, along with her taste, her smell, her sound, her touch. She was imprinted on his soul. "Parting from you won't be easy," he murmured. Hell, the idea of not touching her anymore already seemed like a monumental act of self-denial.

More to prove to himself that he could than out of any desire to do so, he slowly lifted his hand, curling his fingers into a tight fist to keep from putting them right back on her skin. He felt instantly bereft. The slight frown that just as instantly curved her mouth started a small, hot ache in the vicinity of his heart. No, watching Jenna King walk away would not be easy.

And she'd have to walk. It had taken all his will to stop touching her. He didn't think he had enough anywhere inside him to enable him to be the one to leave.

Bob. Rescue Bob. He sighed. The mere idea of trying to haul himself upright again was almost too daunting to contemplate. How much easier and more wonderful it would be to curl up on this nice patch of sun-warmed grass and pull Jenna's sleeping body to nestle against him. . . .

With a restrained groan, T.J. shifted his body.

His mouth twisted into a grimaced smile as he balanced his weight on his good leg and conned his shoulder into helping him use one crutch to pull himself upright. He and Jenna were more alike than she knew.

T.J. carefully edged around Jenna, unable to resist one last peek. He frowned as he saw the return of tension lines to her face. As gratifying as it was to know that his touch could ease her troubles, even if it was only subconsciously, he'd rather she had no troubles at all. Or that she'd share them with him so he could find a way to really help.

He resolutely turned away and made his way toward the baby. First things first.

The first thing he saw when he scanned the open acreage beyond the fence line was salvation.

Not ten feet on the other side was a utility shed tucked up under the pine trees. It was an old plain board building with tin roofing of a decent enough size to hold a tractor at least. But it was what was parked in front of the shed that had caught T.J.'s attention. FARM USE, T.J. read off the hand-painted back plates of the more-rust-than-metal pickup truck. As long as it ran, T.J. didn't much care what it looked like.

"Well, Bob," he said, turning to rub the baby's seeking muzzle. "Looks like in the end, you did the rescuing." Bob simply batted his ridiculously long lashes and nudged T.J.'s hand harder, almost causing him to lose balance. "Whoa now. Just because you're no longer on the dinner menu doesn't mean you can walk all over me." He rubbed the llama's neck as he checked out the situation he'd gotten himself into. The baby hummed in his throat at the attention. "Spoiled brat is what you are," T.J. said distractedly. He was going to need something to cut the wire and some of Bob's fur—which meant finding a way through the fence.

Since Bob was wedged into the fence's only broken-down section, that meant climbing over or through. T.J. sighed. Going through the slats was out. He was simply too big. And he didn't think any amount of bullying was going to convince his body it could manage to climb over.

A sudden moan from behind him drove the dilemma clean from his mind. Jenna. He barely caught himself from spinning around, an action that would have likely sent him sprawling into the coils of rusty barbed wire with Bob. When he did manage to hop around, it was to see Jenna twisting and writhing, making occasional guttural moans that sounded as if someone had reached inside her soul and ripped them from her. T.J. immediately began the awkward trek back to her side, barely thinking clearly enough to speak to the baby when Bob resumed his frantic whines at being abandoned.

"It's okay, it's okay. It'll all be okay." T.J. repeated the litany over and over, knowing it was for all three of them, wishing he could be more convincing. He'd made this promise to her once before. He recalled with vivid clarity her earlier nightmarish episode. Apparently, sleep didn't provide solace from her demons either. *It did when she was in your arms.*

The black mantle of guilt crept in once again, almost choking him this time as he watched her writhe helplessly. He shouldn't have left her, should never have stopped stroking her. He didn't stop to question why it was his responsibility. It simply was.

"Toby, no!" Her strangled howl grabbed at his

throat. She was twisting now, clawing at her shirt and jeans as if they were somehow choking her. "Run!" she screamed hoarsely. "Run, damn you!" Her shout ended in a tortured moan as she continued to writhe, but her movements slowed as racking sobs shook her frame. "Can't save me. Don't. Not like Jonny. Please God, don't . . ."

As he reached her side what seemed like a lifetime later, her sobs had diminished into low, keening moans, her body curled in on itself as she rocked in a relentless to-and-fro pattern.

Heedless of the shriek of pain in his shoulder, he dropped to the ground in a semicontrolled forward fall. There was a popping sound as the splints cracked, and the nausea-inducing feel of something tearing in his knee as he hit the ground momentarily stilled him until he could will the encroaching black void of unconsciousness to recede.

"Jenna," he said softly, touching her face. Flames of pain licked at his shoulder and knee, stars still winked at the periphery of his vision, but he concentrated everything he had on stroking her face, smoothing his shaky fingertips over her hair. "It's okay, baby. It's okay. No one is hurt. We're all okay. You're safe, Jenna, I've got you. You're safe."

Gradually, her rocking slowed, her moans softened to whimpers. T.J. kept on, his entire being focused on her. "One way or the other, we're going to talk about this," he said gently. "You need to get it out." He stroked her face again, then leaned in and placed as soft a kiss as he could on her temple. "You need me."

It was at once that simple and that complicated. Because in that moment he realized he needed her too. He needed her frank approach to situations and her blustery bravado when life approached her a bit too closely. He needed her strong will and determination and her sweet surrender.

But what leveled his remaining defenses was his sudden revelation that even if he let her walk away, he couldn't go back to working for Scottie and the Dozen. His work for them required him to be separate, insular, a loner in heart, mind, and soul. He wasn't a loner any longer.

And without Jenna, he'd simply be alone.

As if he'd relayed his feelings through his touch, her eyelids slowly opened. His mouth was still whisper close. He didn't back away or take his hand away—he couldn't. He continued to stroke her, silently hoping that she'd both drift back to healing sleep . . . and that she'd stay awake and help him explore this new path she'd unknowingly led him down.

She didn't stiffen or pull away. Her eyes were as warm and richly soft as chocolate left in the sun. "You rescued me." Her naturally husky tone blended delectably with the dreamy softness of her whispered declaration.

"I'm beginning to think we rescued each other." Even though he'd barely whispered, his words chased the dreaminess from her eyes as she came fully awake.

"What are you doing?" she asked sharply. Her gaze shifted right and left, then back to his. "Did I fall again?"

T.J. stayed right where he was. "You collapsed after crossing the mudflats."

Her brows furrowed, then smoothed. A tiny bit of color returned to her cheeks. "I think I'm okay. You can back off now." She started to shift to her side, but T.J. stopped her with a hand to her shoulder.

"You had a nightmare, probably brought on by extreme fatigue." He pushed on even as she very deliberately began to shut down. I'm sorry, Jenna, he wanted to say but didn't. He didn't want to hurt her, but he knew if he gave her any opportunity to build new walls, she'd not only seize it, but would find a way to make them more impenetrable than before. He cared too much to let that happen. "Who's Toby?"

If he'd slapped her, Jenna couldn't have been more stunned—or hurt. She felt . . . betrayed. Somehow, somewhere she'd gotten the idea that T.J. wouldn't hurt her. She'd begun to trust him.

You're safe, Jenna, I've got you.

T.J.'s whispered words echoed through her mind. Had he really said them? Or in her fevered dream had she merely wanted him to?

It didn't matter. He'd proven that.

She shoved hard at his chest. It was like trying to move a granite slab. Even if all her strength had been available to her, the outcome would have been the same. It was frustrating. When she pushed, things generally moved. She looked him in the eyes. "It's none of your damn business. Get off me," she demanded, galled that she had to do even that much. "There are ranch buildings a couple hundred yards on the other side of the fence. I want to get there before it starts getting dark." Which would be in a few short hours judging from the slant of the sun behind T.J.'s head.

"We have plenty of time."

"Maybe by your watch. But when the sun dips behind that range, it's going to get real cold, real fast. You may be Superman, but I won't be winning any speed races across that field. Let me up now."

"You won't have to get across the field on foot. There's a farm truck on the other side of the fence. I was trying to free Bob so we could get to it when you began to scream."

"Great, we finally get a break. So why don't—" *Scream?* She'd screamed in her sleep? Heat stung her cheeks as mortification clogged her throat.

"It killed me to hear you like that. Talk to me, Jenna." His tone was velvet smooth, but his voice contained a thread of steel nonetheless. "What happened to you and Toby? Does it have something to do with your ankle?"

Fear ate through the humiliation, investing the words that spewed forth with anger. "For the last time, Delahaye, it's not open for discussion. Get off me. Screaming's not the only way I can kill you."

He smiled. The son of a gun smiled.

Her hand swung up along with her knee. Neither

connected. With a grunt of pain, he pulled her further under him. Despite his cavemanlike tactics, he'd been careful not to hit her ankle. That only made her angrier.

"You get your kicks bullying people?" she ground out.

"No, that's your department."

Her mouth dropped open in shock. Then she remembered her ankle. "And don't coddle me, dammit," she sputtered. She wrestled beneath him, but rolling a redwood off of her would have been easier.

"I love it when you get physical."

Her voice shook with barely leashed fury. "Don't you dare condescend to me either."

"What, can't handle a little real competition, Jenna? Am I getting in too close? Didn't you ever take time to build defenses for that?" He leaned in closer. "Or didn't you think you'd ever need them?"

"You have no idea what I need."

"Oh, but I think I do."

Her eyes widened, and her heart cranked up another few beats per second. "Then you don't know squat. You're no different than the rest of them," she lied. He was nothing like anyone she'd ever met.

"I'm not talking about sex, Jenna. Not that I don't think spending an hour or two exploring your mouth wouldn't be a worthwhile endeavor, not to mention incredibly satisfying . . . but that's not what you need." He had the nerve to wink at her. "At least not all of it."

It galled her to lie there and do nothing, but she

refused to give him the satisfaction of struggling again. Leaving the rage clear in her eyes, she allowed her body to go limp beneath his. It took every ounce of will she had. "Fine, knock yourself out. We'll both freeze our asses off. At least yours will get it first."

"Such a tantalizing invitation." He leaned in closer and let his lips barely brush hers.

Jenna cursed silently when she felt herself tremble in response to his gentle caress and seductive words. If he'd simply taken her mouth hard and brutally, she would have . . . *You would have loved that too*, her little voice said. "Shut up," she muttered. The action made her lips rub against his.

"You're right. Maybe we should stop talking for a while." He took a slow, wet taste of her lips, dipped down and kissed her chin, then dropped tiny, soft kisses at the corners of her mouth. Framing her face with one hand, he leaned into her and continued the assault. How could kisses be both lazy and determined? She felt no pressure, yet there was a definite demand.

Jenna realized far too late how badly she'd misjudged the strength of her defenses against him. Going pliant beneath him had only emphasized how beautifully he fit into the contours of her body. His big body felt heavy and wonderful and matched hers toe to toe, hip to hip. It was a singular experience, and she'd have been worse than a liar if she said she wanted him to get off of her now. She wanted to move under him, press the dark ache that throbbed between her legs against the sweet hard length that was right there for the taking, and certain to ease it.

She wanted to taste him, hold him, run her fingers over every inch of his body, then follow up with her mouth and tongue. She wanted to kiss him.

So she did.

On a soft moan, she opened her mouth and shifted so it covered his. His responding growl sent hot shivers of pleasure over her skin and right straight down through her body. Oh, the power, the beauty, and the pleasure . . . She hadn't known. She hadn't, in her wildest fantasies, imagined it could be like this. They matched. He was perfect for her. She was perfect for him.

The very idea was almost too huge to contemplate. Jenna the Amazon feeling feminine and . . . and . . . And oh, dear sweet Lord but she wanted to take him. Even more thrilling, she wanted to be taken by him. And the darkest, most secret thrill of all was the knowledge that he could take her, fully and completely.

Surrender. Never had she thought there could be power and strength in giving herself to another. Oh, but she'd been wrong, so incredibly, wonderfully wrong.

T.J. plunged his tongue into her mouth, sipping, tasting. Jenna wanted that. So she took it. T.J. groaned into her mouth, causing the urgency of her needs to leap up another level. She slid her tongue down the length of his, then pressed her hip up against him as she wrapped her tongue around his. All of her, around all of him. The feeling was stark and sinous, exhilarating and erotic.

Once understanding of what she was doing snuck in, desire grabbed her hard and fast until she was suddenly desperate to satisfy it. Desperate to have him fill her.

"T.J.," she breathed, pulling in air. Air, she needed air. Instead of panic, it brought the wondrous thrill of danger. The rush of adrenaline was pure and powerful. Only her job had ever given her that, and she'd thought she'd never crave it again. It was a shock to find that heady response with him, in intimacy. Yes, yes, she wanted to shout, exulting in her discovery. There *was* danger here. Yet she was safe to explore it, safe to take her time. Nothing could hurt her. It was all about feelings and pleasure. The only danger lay in what she might discover about herself.

"Oh, you taste good," T.J. said. Her answer was lost on a gasp as he slid his tongue along her jaw and down her throat. He licked her neck, nibbled it, then kissed it.

She arched madly beneath him, half-wild to take what she needed to assuage the clawing ache between her legs. Her writhing incited T.J., who met her hips with a drive of his own. His growl against her neck drove her insane.

She grabbed at his head, spearing her fingers through his hair. "Do something, damn you," she demanded on a hoarse breath.

He lifted his head. His eyes were bright and hot,

and she'd never seen anything so incredible in all her life.

"For God's sake, make this ache go away, T.J." she half begged, half demanded, knowing in her heart of hearts he was more than capable . . . and the only one who could.

He ground his hips down, wringing a long growl from her from deep in her throat. His eyes flared brighter, the smile that crossed his face at once devastatingly wicked and seductive.

"You want me to put your fire out, Jenna?"

The analogy didn't startle her. It was too perfect. "Yes." *Yes, yes, yes.* The word echoed again and again as she pulled his head back down to hers. Her mind raced, her emotions a mad tumble, yet somehow there was a clarity of thought she'd never experienced. Here, she thought with absolute certainty, here all my fires will be tended. Some extinguished forever . . . others stoked again and again to a flaming conflagration.

It was as if he read her thoughts. "What say we fan the flames a little hotter first, my Jenna." He nipped at her mouth, then bit her chin. "Make it more fun to put out." The obvious pleasure he found in her was intoxicating, seemed to beg her to come and play. She couldn't resist or refuse.

A small smile curved her lips, spreading when his pupils shot wider and his breath caught. "I should warn you," she said. "When it comes to fire, you're playing with a professional."

This time T.J.'s grin was on the far side of wicked.

He leaned in and licked a path from her lips to her ear. His whisper was dark and hot and oh so deliciously full of promise. "Go ahead, hotshot, you go on and light my fire." He nipped her earlobe, then pulled it into his mouth.

Jenna whimpered on a strangled laugh. "Dear God, the things you do to me."

He looked back at her. "We've only just begun, my Jenna. We've only just begun." Then he took her.

This time his kiss was hard and demanding. He pressed his weight more fully on her. She kissed him back with everything she had, reveling in the sudden knowledge that, with T.J., she would never need to hold back. She was free to be herself, all of herself. It blew her mind. She attacked with exuberance, reeling with the pleasures of this newfound territory, delighted to find his encouragement at every taste, every touch, every whispered demand.

"That's it. Take me, Jenna. Come and get what you want."

She grabbed his shoulders, and he suddenly stilled, grunting with pain. She froze. "Oh, no, your shoulder. T.J. I'm so sorr—"

With an even deeper growl, he slid his good arm under her and rolled to his back, cutting off her words as he splayed her across his chest with thrilling ease.

Her bad ankle remained safely on the ground, but she immediately swung her other leg wide across him to avoid hitting his knee—which ended up wedging what ached the most right down against the one thing that was sure to ease it.

"Oh . . . my." She stilled, but her hips had other ideas. They rolled, and a cascade of pleasure washed back over her.

T.J.'s answering moan seconded the idea. "That's right, Jenna. You can take that too." He reached up with his good arm to pull her down. "Please."

"Your knee, your shoulder—"

"Are fine compared to this other ache that I have. Come here."

She went willingly against his beautifully bared chest. He cradled her tightly, and it was more satisfying than she'd ever imagined.

"You don't have to hold back with me," he said gently, then tipped her face to his and kissed her long and deep until she was squirming again and wanting to claw her clothes off, and his.

"Mmm-hmm, that's it. Move on me, Jenna. You can't hurt me." She happened to grind down on him at that moment, and he groaned, "God no, you're going to kill me first." He yanked her mouth back to his and took her roughly until they were both breathing hard and writhing. His voice a gravel rasp, he put a whisper of space between their lips and said, "I want to be inside you. I'll fill you up, Jenna. You'll take all of me. We're a match. A perfect match."

T.J. was sure his heart—or something equally important—was going to explode if he didn't feel her wrapped fully around him. He reached down between them and all but ripped the brass stud from his jeans.

He grinned when his fingers tangled with hers. "You do yours, I'll do mine."

TEN

T.J. was rewarded with a breathless laugh that changed to a moan when her zipper slid down. He stopped long enough to enjoy the exquisite sensations that rocked him as she shimmied her jeans down and slipped one leg off.

And then he was free. A second later he did die. She wrapped her hand around him and kissed the exploding pulse on the side of his neck.

"We'd better—you have to—" He choked on his own half groan, half laugh. She'd reduced him to a stuttering, lust-crazed maniac. "Jenna, please, for the love of—"

Then his throat slammed shut as his world went hot. And wet. And so tight. "Dear merciful heaven," he managed between gasps as she slid down the entire length of him.

He held her hips tight when they hit his. He

didn't dare move. He was certain the universe would explode if he did.

"T.J.?" Her voice was muffled against his neck. He couldn't say anything, couldn't have if his life depended on it. Then she pressed the sweetest, most heartbreakingly gentle kiss beneath his ear. His heart melted.

"Come here, Jenna," he managed.

She moved her mouth to his. Compliance, it was a first. And oh, she did pick her moments.

"Look at me."

She lifted her head a fraction. Her eyes were huge and drenched with desire. "Something wrong?"

"No," he choked out. "I wanted you to watch what you do to me. So you know." He kissed her, then nudged her head back up again. "Move, Jenna."

"What?"

"Move on me, against me."

She tightened her thighs, and he thought his eyes were going to roll up into his head.

"Like that?"

"Yeah," he said through clenched teeth. "Sort of like that."

She moved again. He groaned.

"I'm not hurting you?"

"Uh-uh." It was all he could get out.

She moved a bit more. He died a bit more. "So this feels good?"

It took an incredible amount of concentration to form a coherent syllable. "Yes."

"And this?" she asked, all sweet unrelieved innocence as she rotated her siren hips.

At some point he'd shut his eyes, because he had to wink one open to look at her face. She was smiling.

"Like this," he said with a growl. He pulled her down, clamped one arm across her back, and thrust up once, as hard and deep as he could.

"Oh, yes," she cried on a long hiss of approval, and instantly convulsed around him.

"Yeah, yes," he said on an equally blissful hiss, and came long and hard.

Jenna's body shuddered as T.J. pulsed inside her, wave after wave of wrenching sensation twisting her tighter, filling her, electrifying her. She didn't ever want it to end. In fact, she discovered she wanted more. It was as if some button long buried had finally been pushed, and she would do almost anything to keep the pressure directly on it.

She moved on him, eliciting what sounded like a half curse, half moan when she felt him respond.

"I still need you," she said, hearing the wonder in her voice. She liked it. Loved it.

He pushed back when she moved again. "I can't imagine not always needing more of you," he said, then found her mouth and took her there again.

This time it was fast and hard with both of them thrusting and driving. Now that the almost crippling ache was gone, she could deepen the pleasure, enjoy it, take it even higher. And he accommodated her all the way. They thrust in perfect unison, going harder and faster as if testing to see if the other truly was their match.

Neither faltered. And then, as if by mutual agreement, they would relax, and T.J. would stroke excruciatingly slowly, wringing exquisite sensation from every inch inside her.

"Never," he breathed at one point.

"Never what?" she managed, rocking hard against him, building the fury.

"Never, no one, only you . . ." He kissed her neck and drew in one ragged breath, then another. He met her moves even as his gaze silently commanded hers. "You were made for me, Jenna King. Only you. You're mine."

Jenna squeezed her eyes shut as he drove into her. After all their primal sparring, it only took one . . . again. This time, as she shuddered around him, pulling him deeper, she silently acknowledged that his truth was also hers.

There was only T.J. And he was hers.

They must have slept, because it was his lips pressing gentle kisses on her forehead that woke her up. The steady throb in her ankle was a distant concern. She was nestled against him, on top of him. Nestled. She rubbed her face against his sun-warmed skin. Funny, she thought, in all their frenzy of lovemaking, there was still so much of him yet to explore.

A hot thrill stole over her, robbing her momentarily of breath, stilling her. It was all so new, so incredible and unbelievably scary. But she wanted it as she had wanted nothing and no one ever before. She wanted this. Him. There was no turning away from her feelings. They consumed her even as they frightened her.

But it was a direction, and she so badly needed one. Whatever it might cost her later didn't matter. He mattered. And as she had done with everything else in her life that mattered, she would fight like hell for it. For him.

She also knew that a path had to be taken one step at a time. With a trip in her heart that was a mingling of excitement and trepidation, she lifted her head, looked at T.J. . . . and took that first step.

"Toby was my partner. He died saving my life."

T.J.'s lips and hands stilled. He hadn't known what to expect when she awoke, but her quiet declaration would have been far down on the list. After he'd let it sink in, he realized the dual importance of her offering. She was letting him in, purposely opening the door. And she'd only do that if she cared. He silently rejoiced.

His mind had been running on an endless wheel as she slept curled on top of him. Still rocked by the mind-numbing sensations she'd wrung from his body, he'd found himself assaulted by emotions he could put no name to. Even as the feverish responses of his body subsided, the feelings in his head, and in his heart, continued to wreak havoc.

He combed his fingers through her hair, lightly pressing her head to his chest as he rested his chin there. The silence spun out, as did the tension, but it wasn't entirely unpleasant. It was more a matter of anticipation. Down deep inside, where emotions and feelings he'd never expected to have were slowly uncurling, he understood that what happened next between them would likely create the foundation for the most important stage of his life. He was at once terrified and exhilarated.

Choosing his words carefully, he finally spoke. "I know what it's like to lose a partner."

She'd been tracing aimless patterns on his chest with her fingertips. The motion stilled. There were several seconds of complete quiet, even their breathing seemed momentarily suspended, then, in a subdued voice that sounded nothing like the Jenna King he was falling in love with, she said, "Was it your fault?"

His breath returned on a sharp intake. He made a conscious effort to even it out before replying. "No. But that didn't stop the guilt."

Another long pause. "Will you tell me what happened?" The instant the question was out, she started to move, to pull away.

Her actions caused him to slide out of her, eliciting a dismayed gasp from her that melted his heart.

"Never mind," she said quickly. "I had no right to—"

He clamped his arm around her and held her tight. "Shh. You had every right." When he felt her relax against him, he released her, then tipped her head back. Her eyes were steeped in a myriad emotions, not all of them nameable. But the ones he could identify strengthened his determination to make this woman his. He could live forever in those eyes of hers.

"You can ask me anything, Jenna. Always." When he saw the walls building, he added, "I don't *have* to answer, you know." He laid a finger on her lips to still her immediate response. "But I choose to. Just as you chose to talk to me. We always have a choice." He slid his finger away, letting it linger on her lower lip a second or two, then drop away as he sighed. "I know I tried to pressure you earlier, because I thought it would help you. I still think it will. I don't mind sharing if it will make it easier on you; I don't mind sharing anything with you, period. But it's your choice. I only want you to do this if you're ready, not because you think you owe it to me. I'll always be ready to listen."

What he saw in her eyes now was gratitude, which warmed him like no amount of sunshine ever could.

"I don't think I'll ever be ready," she said, her rough voice even huskier than usual. "But I do want to talk about it. Or maybe need is a better word."

She ducked her head, and he cradled it back against his chest. A quick check of the sun told him they still had a little time before the temperatures really began to drop. He was willing to lie out there all night, half-naked, in subzero temperatures, if that's what she needed.

"I'd just as soon never think about it again as long as I live," she said quietly. "But I have to face the fact that my subconscious does, or it wouldn't torture me with the whole mess every time I shut my eyes."

"Did they counsel you at Paradise?" He smiled as he felt her grimace against his chest. This was the Jenna he loved. Somewhere in his mind he noted that this was the second time he had thought of love in conjunction with his feelings for Jenna, but he pushed that away. For now.

"I think they worked harder trying to rehab my head than they did my leg and ankle."

"Your leg?"

"I suffered some third-degree burns on the area above where my ankle was crushed. I had some skin grafts that required special care. They're pretty much healed now."

He studied her for several silent moments. It was obvious she expected some form of interrogation. It was a reaction he might deserve, but she was about to learn that in this case, he wasn't the man she expected him to be, but the man she needed him to be.

"Sometimes it's the wounds you can't see that are the hardest to heal," he said quietly.

She splayed her palm flat on his chest and pressed, as if to absorb his heartbeat. He would have ripped it out and handed it to her if he thought it would help. It already belonged to her anyway.

To his surprise, she smiled. "How did someone as obnoxious and clutzy as you get to be so wise?" she said, but there was far more tenderness in her tone than sarcasm.

Another piece of his soul slipped away, and he let it go willingly. "Dumb luck."

He felt her small chuckle. "Uh-huh. Dumb like a fox."

He continued to trace his fingers lightly through her hair, letting his mind wander to images of untwining the heavy braid and watching it fall all over her shoulders . . . or spread out on his pillow. Of course, in his line of work, sleeping on his own pillow was a rare thing. . . . He pushed all of those thoughts away. He was right where he wanted to be. His main concern and sole focus was Jenna. He'd sort the rest out later.

"So I gather they didn't help you?"

She sighed. "Some," she admitted, then, with more conviction, she added, "Of course, that they didn't do more is probably my fault."

"I can't imagine," T.J. said dryly, and was rewarded with a small pinch. "Hey," he said, not minding in the least. The lady didn't pull any punches or take any grief but was well prepared to dish out both. He liked that. "Oh, so you're saying you were a model patient and willing subject?"

There was a pause and the sound of a muffled snort followed by a very dignified sniff. Then she peeked up at him, but after less than a second her solemn expression gave way to a mischievous grin. "Wouldn't know how if I tried."

"Naturally, this came as such a shock to those who know and love you." Of which he was one, he thought, surprised by the restraint he had to use to not voice it.

Her smile faded, becoming small and sad, dragging his down with it. He tightened his hold on her.

"Actually, no," she said softly. "My parents alternately begged and ordered me to be more cooperative. They weren't surprised by my attitude."

"I gathered earlier that you aren't exactly close to them, but surely they understood the enormity of what you were dealing with?"

There had been so much to tell, to explain, to work through, yet suddenly Jenna couldn't find a single word to say. He still knew very little about what had actually happened, yet, in that one statement, uttered so simply, with such unquestioning certainty, she'd heard the one thing that no one else had been able to convey: understanding. It was an indefinable, yet crucial difference she'd never been able to pinpoint. But it was there in his voice, behind his words.

"My therapist has counseled a number of people dealing with what she termed misplaced guilt," Jenna finally said. "So she thought she knew. She didn't. It hadn't happened to *her*." Her voice shook with emotion as she uttered the last words, surprising her with its intensity. And like a snap of the fingers, it was as if a logjam had broken loose inside her. There was suddenly this tremendous tidal wave of words and feelings, bottlenecked for what felt like centuries, all begging for release at once. It took all her willpower to tame them into intelligent phrases, to speak slowly and clearly, instead of giving in to the force of raw emotion. If she did, it would spill out all over him in a rush of overwhelming relief because there was finally, at long last, someone she trusted enough to tell.

"Jenna, you—"

His quiet words had her realizing she was indeed clutching him, digging her ragged fingernails into the solid strength of his chest. "It's—it's okay." She consciously relaxed her hands. *Slow down, there's plenty of time*, she schooled herself. *He'll be here to listen. He will listen.* She took a steadying breath.

"My parents lost a son, so they—" She broke off as a deep ache welled up in her throat and put a hitch in her voice. She cleared it and pushed on, knowing with some unexplainable certainty that if she ever hoped to reclaim full control of her head and her heart, it was this man who would help her navigate the way. Only this man.

"They . . . they thought that what they'd gone through put them in the position to understand what I was dealing with. But they . . . they . . ." She pressed a hand to her mouth to stifle a sudden sob. She never cried, never allowed herself to cry, not anymore, not about this. Closing her eyes tightly against the hot threat of tears, she fought hard for composure. On some level she knew that she needed to get through her past to get to the rest. And she desperately needed to get throught the rest.

T.J.'s fingers never stopped stroking her, soothing her, giving her the rhythm of solace to focus on, cling to. His gentle understanding and easy silence brought tears to her eyes from another place inside her soul. It also gave her the strength to continue.

"My brother Jonny died in a fire on our ranch when I was fifteen," she said, her voice shaking. "He was only eleven. It wasn't anybody's fault, an electrical storm triggered it, set a barn full of hay on fire. But I . . . I was in the barn . . . had been in the barn. It was late at night, and I wasn't supposed to be out there, but my mare had foaled that morning and I wanted to spend some time alone with her and the baby. Jonny knew where I was, because I'd told him to cover for me in case Mom or Dad checked on us, and he . . . he . . ." She took a rough breath and swallowed hard on the growing knot in her throat. "He tried to save me, but I had already led my mare and the baby out the back. The front loft was consumed, and it collapsed almost immediately. He had run in screaming for me right as it . . . and he was . . . oh God. I didn't know he would . . . didn't think—"

She had to stop when her throat closed over. But while the horrifying images of that night, of the fire, of the destruction of her family, of her life, blazed to roaring life in her mind's eye, instead of the paralyzing fear and racking guilt that usually gripped her, a deep aching tide of pain and sorrow surged through her.

"It's okay, Jenna. Let it out."

It was only when she heard T.J.'s smooth deep voice reaching out to her, through the pain, that she realized she was crying. Deep, wrenching sobs shook her entire body . . . but began to heal her soul.

He held her tight and continued to stroke her, slow and steady. "I'm sorry for your family," he said softly, his words barely audible. "I never had brothers or sisters. My folks died in a car accident while I was in Canada visiting my grandfather. That was hard enough. I can't imagine dealing with something like this."

"If I hadn't . . . been there . . ." she managed on sharp, ragged breaths. "I shouldn't . . . have . . . been—"

"Cry for him, Jenna," T.J. interrupted, his tone still gentle but firm. "What happened is a horrible thing. Miss him like hell. You'll miss him forever. Remember him, it's how you honor who he was, how special and important he was. But don't beat yourself with his death. Yes, you feel guilty, anyone would. But you didn't do anything to deliberately put him or anyone else in danger. No one could have known what would happen. You both made choices. His had tragic consequences."

Even as some deep-down-where-it-counts part of her latched onto his words, heard them and believed them, she fought it. Decades of blame weren't easily erased or given up. "But he died because of me," she said, lifting her head to look at him. "Because of me, T.J."

She looked so bewildered and lost, T.J. thought his heart would break. "No, Jenna," he said softly. "He died trying to save you. He loved you. You would have done the same for him. Would you have blamed him if the tables were turned? No," he answered for her. "You'd be the first one to say that you made your own decision, did what you thought you had to do. Right?" Again he didn't wait for her to answer, but he could see she was thinking about it, really listening to what he was saying.

"Let me ask you another question."

She sniffed, her eyes glassy with tears, her eyelids swollen, hiccuping air into lungs aching with grief. He knew at that instant he truly loved her. With all of his heart, he would always love her.

"What?" she managed.

"If you'd been in the house when lightning struck and seen the fire, would you have tried to save your mare and her baby?"

"Of course I would."

"And if you'd raced in as the loft collapsed . . . Would you have blamed the horses? Would you expect anyone to blame them?"

She didn't respond. But he saw she didn't need to.

He leaned down and kissed her forehead, the tip of his nose, then her mouth. "It's hard to accept that other people can make decisions that might hurt them, even kill them, and you can't do anything about it. Especially if you had anything to do with what motivated the decision."

He kissed her again, then lifted his head and smiled. "Like you couldn't keep me from almost breaking my neck to save you. You sure as hell didn't blame that on yourself."

Her brow furrowed again, and his heart stopped. For a split second he wanted to kill himself for taking it one step too far. She was in so much pain, facing some very tough truths, and he couldn't bully her any longer. He would never forgive himself if she took to heart what he'd meant as a joke. "Jenna," he warned. Her expression smoothed, and a small tentative smile curved her lips.

"True," she said. "That was your own stupid fault."

He was still concerned.

"God, but I'm a jinx," she said, her breath still hitching.

He knew she'd meant to sound sarcastic, but she missed the boat by a mile. He cupped her head and turned it to his. Sternly, he said, "Jenna, you do not control the lives of those around you. They get to make their own choices about what they do. And it's their choices, not yours, that determine their fate."

"I know, I know," she said, and he believed her. He closed his eyes on a sigh of relief.

When he opened them she was regarding him steadily. "I do understand, T.J. In my head I always have. But in my heart . . ." She looked away for a second, then pulled her gaze back to him, as if it were something she had to do. There was determination in her eyes again and something else that— She dipped her chin and kissed the spot where his heart was beating.

"*You* understand, T.J. In your head *and* your heart. I wish for your sake you didn't, because it means you went through the same sort of hell I did. But somehow you came out of it whole. And you've shown me the way to make myself whole. I can't tell you what that means. It's . . . there's more. About Toby. About me. A lot more. But I think I can begin to deal with that too. It's . . . T.J., I can't . . ." She sniffed, and he watched her swallow hard against renewed tears. "It's the most tremendous gift, and I have no way to thank you that can do it justice."

"You did all that and more with your kiss," he said gruffly, his own eyes suddenly burning. "Come here, Jenna." He pulled her up until her face was even with his. "I'm glad I helped you. I'll listen to all of it, whatever you need to tell me. I'll do whatever it takes. I don't want to see you hurting anymore." He cupped her head close until their lips were close to touching. "For right now, kiss me." He brushed his lips against hers. "We've had enough hurt. It's time for some pleasure. There has to be pleasure too."

ELEVEN

Jenna wanted badly to sleep, but she kept her gaze trained on the rearview mirror. It was warped and the glass was cracked, but she could still make out Bob, trailing behind the pickup truck as they slowly drove to the small cluster of outbuildings.

Freeing Bob had required her to shimmy on her back under the fence to look in the equipment shed for something to cut him loose with. They'd caught one minor break when she found a large box in the back of the dilapidated farm truck that contained fence-repair supplies, including a pair of wire cutters. Bob had come through minus some fur, but without a scratch. She couldn't say the same for herself. Images of T.J.'s face, sweet and teasing, dark with desire, taut with pain, swam through her mind.

She wanted to sleep. Not think. Her body was well past exhausted, but her mind wouldn't shut down. So much had happened in the last twelve hours, and it all buzzed in her head like a swarm of bees, each of which had something equally important to say. If she could rest for a while, she could begin to put everything together, begin to sort the chaos into some semblance of order so she could figure out what she was going to do with the rest of her life.

She glanced at T.J., as she had done frequently, whether she chose to or not. His face was drawn in a tight grimace and weary fatigue lines bracketed his mouth and eyes, replacing the ones of warmth and humor. Once again she was stunned by how he'd put his own pain aside and focused on helping her. Her skin heated again and her pulse quickened, making her want to groan. She was too tired to have her heart beat even a second faster. But thoughts of his arms around her, his mouth on hers, him driving inside her— *Enough!* She couldn't deal with this now.

It had been a pivotal moment in her life, joining herself to this man. But what had followed had been even more profound. He'd guided her through her guilt and misery, showing her the path out. Monumental. She found herself studying him yet again. Simply looking at him brought on a rush of emotion that should have terrified her.

Instead she felt . . . safe. He provided a peaceful, gentle, yet indestructible sense of security. That's what she'd found; in his arms, in his eyes, in his words, in his actions. She couldn't be terrified. There was a rightness to him, to being with him. It went deeper than feeling or thought, she couldn't completely explain it, but nevertheless she knew on a fundamental level the link existed, without questions or exceptions. And always would.

A sensation of pure wonder rushed over her, sizzling and snapping along her every nerve ending, the message undeniable.

She was falling in love with T. J. Delahaye.

"Uh-oh." T.J.'s dire tone yanked her from that stunning revelation like nothing else could have.

His expression had her turning to look forward. A couple of small barns loomed directly in front of them. "What's wrong?"

"No activity. The whole place looks abandoned." He pulled around the largest barn. "I wonder wha—" He broke off on a whispered expletive as Jenna inhaled sharply.

"Fire," they both said.

Bile rose in her throat, hard and unexpected. On some level, she knew the reaction was due to her having so recently relived her childhood experiences on her parents' ranch. Still, the force of the reaction bothered her. She pressed a hand to her stomach and took a slow, steady breath, quelling the riot in her stomach even as she forced herself to survey the area.

"Treetops are gone higher up. Looks like a canopy fire that took to the ground once it crossed the ridge," she said without thinking. "Winds were bad this summer. We had these in my region too."

T.J. stopped the truck and turned his head toward her. She kept her gaze forward, suddenly realizing what she'd unthinkingly revealed. She waited for the inevitable questions, her rocky stomach pitching lightly again. She knew she should have expected this, she even wanted to talk to him about it. About Toby. Maybe she'd spoken out loud on purpose.

She pressed her hands more firmly on her abdomen, as if the action would still the thoughts rocking her mind along with the anxiety unsettling her stomach.

After what felt like an eternity, he shifted his gaze to the front. All he said was, "Looks like the building on this side and the house escaped damage."

Jenna nodded, trying to quell the huge sigh of relief that eased from her. He truly understood. She'd known he did, but he'd proven it again by backing off when she needed him to. "They were lucky," she said, thinking all the while that she was the lucky one. She turned her attention back to the ranch. The burned-out ridge that had bordered the creek slanted northward, opening up into the narrow valley. The creek also wended its way across the ranch, a dividing line between destruction and salvation. On the other side of the creek, acre upon acre of ground was blackened, scorched, littered with the remains of other ranch buildings and backed by the ridge dotted with charred pine stumps. "Looks like they saved their biggest buildings, but the rest, along with almost all of their grazing land, is gone."

Bob wandered up to the passenger window. Jenna looked at him as he surveyed his surroundings, and his long lashes blinked slowly several times. He was only an animal, but there was something infinitely sad in that gaze. It made her throat ache.

Suddenly she couldn't bear it another second. She popped the handle and swung the door open, barely missing Bob.

"Where are you going?"

Jenna ground her teeth against the constant pain as she slid her good foot to the ground. "Bob needs food and water."

"So do we."

Bracing her weight against the side of the truck, she retrieved her crutches from the back. "Come on, Bob." The rusty cab door squealed as she shoved it shut.

"Jenna—"

"I need to take care of him first," she said, her sharp tone daring him to disagree. She looked through the open window at T.J., wanting to be angry, needing to be angry. She was dead tired and had serious doubts about her ability to remain upright beyond the next five seconds. Anger was the only reserve of energy she had left to call on.

The tender concern on T.J.'s face fueled it, but it was the understanding that shone from his eyes and voice as he nodded and said, "Do what you have to do," that ended up being the well of strength she drew from.

A rush of emotions flooded her, almost undoing her. As she looked at him feelings of love, tenderness, and a desire so pure she had no idea how to channel it, poured from her head to her heart and straight into her soul. It was all she could do to keep from sliding to the ground in a heap.

She was trembling from her shoulders to her knees, the reaction due to far more than fatigue. She wanted to open the door and crawl across the seat and into his lap and the warm circle of his arms where she knew everything would be okay. She, who had made a career out of strength and will and taking care of herself, wanted nothing more than to beg T. J. Delahaye to take care of her. For the first time she wanted—needed—to share the load.

But she couldn't. She'd started this and she would damn well finish it. Bob was her responsibility, and she had to prove to herself she could still handle one. Straightening her spine and doing her best to coerce her muscles into steady compliance, she managed to nod stiffly, keeping her lips clamped together in a firm line.

He stared at her for a long moment. The gathering shadows of early evening didn't hide the sharp intensity of his gaze or the very real promise he'd made no effort to hide. "I'm going to go to the house and see if we can get in. I'll come back for you."

She had no idea what to say. She turned toward the barn.

"I'll come back for you, Jenna."

He should have had to yell to be heard over the recalcitrant engine. He hadn't, and yet his velvet-soft words enveloped her anyway, surrounding her as surely as his arms would, with warmth and comfort. Amazing, she thought, her throat aching again. She paused, wanting to turn or even lift a hand in acknowledgment, but she was running on empty and even that tiny effort suddenly seemed too much.

"Go on," he called. "I'll be back."

She nodded again, less stiffly this time, and resumed her controlled stumble toward the barn. It wasn't until she'd reached the cool, dank interior that she realized she was smiling. He truly *was* amazing. *So what are you going to do about it?* her inner voice queried. Tell him, was the immediate answer. Her smile grew.

Bob's warm nose nudged her shoulder, jolting her from her thoughts. "Yeah, yeah," she said, but the words were gentle. "You're home." As she said the words she had the feeling that somehow, she had come home too. "Let's find you some food," she continued, her voice a note huskier than usual. Energy from a new well sprang open inside her, infusing her with warmth and strength. As she followed the llama deeper into the shadowed barn interior, she realized the new source was hope. In that moment she thought she could do anything.

Probably delirious from lack of food, water, and sleep, she told herself, but her smile remained. She paused at a stall door. The sensation of homecoming took root and grew rapidly. Familiar smells, familiar feelings . . . She half expected to see a horse lean his head out from one of the stalls. Her heart tightened as memories flooded her. She didn't analyze them, but she didn't resist them either.

Balancing her weight, she reached out and rubbed Bob's neck. He hummed deep in his throat. "What do you guys eat?" As she looked at him her heart felt lighter than it had in what seemed like aeons. "And first thing tomorrow, you're getting a bath. I hate to be the one to tell you this, but Bob ol' buddy, you stink."

T.J. drove the truck around the entire house, over grass, gravel, and dirt. It wasn't the most thorough investigation, but it was the only one his body could manage at the moment. Neat and tidy, he decided, but definitely abandoned. He could get them in, no problem. Of course in his current condition, it would be easier if there was a door or ground-floor window unlocked somewhere. The front door caught his attention. Or more specifically, the small lock on the door handle caught his attention. He groaned.

The property was evidently for sale. There was no sign in the yard, but maybe there was one at the end of the winding drive. He couldn't see that far.

He debated briefly whether to get out now and find a way in or go back for Jenna. At his current rate of speed even a simple B&E might take some time. Jenna would be done by then, and he knew damn well she wouldn't wait for him to pick her up. That meant he picked her up first. He'd worry later how to explain his entry methods and where he'd learned them. And he knew he'd have to. No way would Jenna wait patiently in the truck.

He was halfway across the open space between house and barn before he faced the fact that he wasn't really upset about being put in the position of explaining what he did for a living, who he was. In fact, he was actually almost looking forward to it. Another step down this new path. He took it with anticipation and not a little dread. In there somewhere was also a sense of relief, as if after years of wandering the globe, he'd finally found what he'd been searching for. Quite a shock for a man who'd never been aware that he was looking in the first place. The irony that he'd ended up right back where he'd started from didn't escape him either.

The sight of Jenna slowly dragging herself away from the barn zapped those thoughts from his head. His heart squeezed painfully at the sight of her. She was leaning so heavily on her makeshift crutches, T.J. was surprised she was still upright. Bob was nowhere to be seen, so she'd apparently found a place for him.

He'd known better than to argue with her earlier, no matter how hard it had been to drive away. A blind man could see her last thread had unraveled some time ago. But he'd already learned what the determination he'd seen in her eyes meant, and he respected it. She'd needed to do this. Her choice. No matter how hard it was for him, he'd had to let her follow through on it.

He pressed a little harder on the gas, though the result was marginal. The truck barely functioned. But it would serve its purpose. If he could get the damn thing to Jenna before she collapsed. He wasn't sure he had the strength to pick her up if she did.

As he got closer he saw that her gaze was focused

rigidly on the ground in front of her. He was almost beside her before she looked up. Even determination couldn't overcome the vacant glaze he saw in her eyes. He pulled up so the passenger door was even to her. His shoulder screamed, but he leaned over and shoved at the door handle.

"Can you get in?"

"Of course I can," she shot back, but the retort was barely audible. She managed to get the door open wide enough, but the balance necessary to toss her crutches in the back and climb in seemed beyond her current capacities.

Twice his hand hit his own door handle, though he had no idea what he could do at this point to help her. Even though he'd released the seat all the way back before getting in, he was beginning to realize there was a decent chance that when he unwedged his now unsplinted leg from the cab and stood upright, the resulting rush might black him out. He was damn sure he could only do it once. "Jenna—"

She leaned heavily on the frame of the open door, lifting one hand enough to shush him. "I can do it. Stop rushing me."

If he hadn't been so worried and at the end of his own rope, he'd have chuckled, if for no other reason than to spur her into finishing the task. *Ah, Jenna, my sweet, stubborn, determined love.* He didn't fight the emotions this time, the warmth and energy were too vital.

"The house is empty, but in good shape," he said, giving her something to focus on while she drummed up the will to lever herself into the truck. "They've got it up for sale and are apparently actively showing it, so we might get lucky and have heat and water."

With a long groan she hauled herself into the truck. T.J. reached out and grabbed her arm, helping her in.

"Right now I'd settle for anything flat and stable with a roof over it."

T.J. caught the wince and saw her clenched jaw as she shifted frontward, settling herself, before letting her head tilt back on a long sigh.

"Home, James." A weary grin tilted the corners of her mouth. Eyes closed, she added, "Or Jefferson, as the case may be."

If there were such things as heartstrings, she'd knotted his up so tightly, he knew he'd never untangle them. Just as he knew he wasn't the least bit interested in trying. What he wanted was to find a way to wind hers up just as tightly. He stared at her, wonder racing neck and neck with fear. How could she have already come to mean so much to him? And even more terrifying: what if he didn't mean as much to her?

Her skin was so pale, the setting sun cast the angles of her face in stark relief, the brush of pale lashes against her cheek making her look fragile, yet he found his mouth curving. "Right you are, madam," he intoned in perfect imitation of a proper British chauffeur. Before the truck had rolled ten feet, she was asleep. "Right you are, indeed," he added softly. *Right for me.*

When Jenna opened her eyes, it was full dark. It took her a startled moment to recall where she was. In the truck. As her eyes adjusted, the looming shadow in front of her became the house. The angle of the roof blocked the moon, but she doubted it was too long past sundown. She shivered as awareness of the chilled air seeped through her shirt and into her consciousness at the same time. It was at that moment that she realized two things: she was alone, and she'd slept without having nightmares.

She squinted and peered into the inky depths of the covered porch that extended along the front and wrapped around the side of the house. It was too dark to see anything. She debated what to do.

She knew T.J. was likely trying to find a way into the house. She didn't care if he smashed a window at this point. She'd pay for it. Surely no one would begrudge them shelter after the day they'd had. She also knew that he wouldn't leave her in the truck once he'd accomplished his task.

Which left her two options: wait for him, or get out and try to help him. She wasn't sure how much help she could be, but waiting in the truck didn't sit well with her. Another possibility hit her, eliciting a groan as she sat up straighter and inadvertently pushed her foot against the floorboards. What she wouldn't do for a warm bath, an ice pack, and a bottle of aspirin. But her mind returned immediately to her other thought. What if T.J. *couldn't* come back for her?

The more she thought about it, the more she realized how probable the chances were. His knee was shot. It had been hard for him to make it to the truck, and that was after they'd cut Bob loose, freeing up a wide opening in the fence he could walk through. He'd kept it clamped down, but she'd known the pain he'd endured while removing the brace and getting into the truck. It was very likely he was out there somewhere, lying on the cold ground, unable to get up. Her hand hit the door handle as images of his big body sprawled on the ground, frozen and in considerable pain, assaulted her. Adrenaline pumped into her ragged system, making her almost dizzy.

Just as she shoved the door open a light inside the house blinked on, followed by the front porchlight.

She jerked her head up, then sagged back against the seat as the black shadow of a body emerged at the stop of the wide porch stairs. Backlit, there was no way to make out the face, but that overlarge rugged frame could belong to only one man. "T.J.," she said on a sigh of relief. Then she realized he was going to try to negotiate the stairs and moved quickly to poke her head out of the door.

"Don't you dare come down those stairs," she called out. "You'll end up busting your other knee. Are you crazy?"

"I must be to think about rescuing a stubborn woman like you from a night spent in a broken-down truck in freezing temperatures." It could have been midnight, and she'd still have seen the gleam of his grin.

Her own mouth twitched, but she kept her tone stern. "And how many times do I have to tell you I don't need rescuing?" Even as she spoke she moved to get out. She wasn't chancing him attempting those stairs. She faltered when she put her weight on her good leg and her knee refused to support her.

"Jenna!"

She gripped at the door frame and leaned against the seat, then swiveled her head toward him. "Stay there!" she puffed out as she waited for the blood flow to finish stabbing her leg and foot with hot prickly needles. She refused even to think about her hands. They'd been beyond pain for some time now. When she could finally balance, she stood, then, holding the edge of the truck bed, took a test hop, then another. She retrieved her crutches, but as she placed them in front of her she froze. Suddenly the thought of propping the rough, busted branch nubs under her arms and leaning her body weight on the tender bruised flesh there was simply too much. She'd endured racking, mind-numbing pain. In comparison, another couple feet or so on the crutches should have been nothing. But in that instant it was everything.

She'd hit the wall. Hot tears humiliated her further by stinging the corners of her eyes.

"Jenna?"

Her throat burned with the effort to stop the threatening tears from flowing. If she spoke at all, he'd hear them in her voice. She didn't dare look at him. She stared helplessly at her crutches. She was less than a dozen yards from shelter, and she simply couldn't do it. Anger, pride, humiliation, embarrassment, even hope didn't rush in to save her one last time. She stood there, shaking, knowing it was time to ask for help but unable to find the words. He needed help too. It wasn't fair of her to ask.

Her throat, ravaged from constriction, finally could stand it no more. As it relaxed its chokehold tears coursed down her cheeks. Her leg shook so hard, she dropped the crutches and slumped against the open truck door, hitching her arm through the open window to keep from falling.

"T.J., I can't do this," she finally admitted, her shaky confession barely reaching her own ears. "I . . . I need help."

Strong arms snaked around her waist from behind. "I've got you, Jenna."

If she hadn't already been crying, she would have wept, whether in relief or shame she wasn't entirely sure. "I thought I told you to stay on the porch," she said, but the choking retort had no sting, and when he leaned against the truck and turned her around, she went willingly into his embrace. "I shouldn't have asked. I tried to make it . . . but I couldn't."

He cupped the back of her head, and she didn't hesitate to burrow her face against his flannel-covered chest. In some distant part of her mind she realized he must have found a shirt in the house.

"Shh," T.J. whispered against her hair as he stroked his fingers down her back. "I've been there,

Jenna. Pushed beyond the limit. You're tapped out. Most people couldn't have held out this long."

There was no censure in his tone. He wouldn't tell her she shouldn't have taken care of Bob or criticize any of her other decisions because he respected her choices. He would be there no matter what. She also realized something else. He'd respect her decisions, but his respect for her extended to believing she'd ask for help when she needed it.

As if he'd read her mind, he said, "Everyone needs help at some point. There is no shame in asking."

Her tears subsided as quickly as they'd come, but they left her feeling even more wrung out, something she hadn't thought possible. "You need help too," she said thickly.

"If there had been anyone else to ask, you would have. At that moment I had one more straw left than you."

His arm tightened around her as she lifted her head to look at him. "Asking for help is hard for me, harder than it should be. You have an incredible way of making it okay." She thought of her dream-free nap in the truck. "You've made a lot of things okay for me. When I woke up this morning, all I knew was that I had to get out. I thought that by leaving Paradise I was taking back control of my life. But I was just looking for another place to hide." She reached up and kissed him softly on the lips. "Thank you for not letting me hide, T.J."

He held her so tightly, she would have thought he'd pushed himself beyond his remaining strength, but she was close enough to see his eyes. What she saw there made her shiver.

He lowered his mouth and kissed her, starting out gently but taking it deeper as she responded. She had no words for what he made her feel. Even love didn't do it justice. So she poured all of it into her kiss. He answered her with all that and more.

When he finally lifted his head, she thought they both might simply float into the house.

T.J. stared into her eyes, then carefully drew her battered hands up between them. "It was inside you all along. You're an incredible woman, Jenna. I want you in ways I never thought I'd want anyone."

"I . . . I feel the same way," she said, almost breathless with the wonder of that truth.

He dropped another soft kiss on her lips and a small groan escaped his lips when she started to respond, but he lifted his mouth from hers. "We're both busted up, and yet it's all I can do not to take you right to the ground, right here."

She swallowed hard, a new ache spreading, tightening deep within her. This pain was delicious, especially since her body already knew what the cure felt like. Busted up or not . . . "I can't think of a better way to escape pain," she said. "Why don't we get inside and—"

He shushed her with a quick kiss and shook his head. "I would in a heartbeat if I could. But there's not much time, and there are things I need to tell you."

She pulled her hands from his. "What? I don't understand."

"I work for the government, or at least I did when I came here. For the last ten years I've been part of a team that specialized in handling problems no other authorized organization could—"

"When you said you rescued people, I thought you were an emergency technician or something." She stared at him. "You're telling me you're a . . . a secret agent?"

He searched her eyes as if trying to discover how she felt about his confession, but finally scraped together a tired version of his killer grin. "That's me. Secret agent man."

Why he was telling her now? She was admittedly intrigued. Secret agent? She wanted to know everything about the man she was falling in love with. But something about his urgency was ringing warning bells in her head. "Who . . . whom—whatever—do you rescue?"

"Occasionally, our missions include liberating people from situations that no one else is authorized to handle." He paused, but when she said nothing, he quickly went on. "But what I wanted to tell you is that I'm thinking about retiring. Actually, I guess I've already decided. I just have to tell Scottie. She's my boss. An amazing woman, she's—" He stopped and smiled. "I'll just say that you two would love each other."

Information was coming too fast for her to make

sense of it all. "Retire? Your boss is a woman? Named Scottie?"

He didn't give her a chance to catch up. "I'm pretty sure this knee injury has ruled out fieldwork for me. I can't see myself behind a desk, and I'd make a lousy instructor."

"I think you'd be a wonderful teacher," she said, then shook her head in confusion. "But why is it so important that you tell me all of this now?"

A distant siren wail echoed across the valley.

"That's why."

"The sirens?"

"They're for us. I figure we have about ten minutes before they get here."

TWELVE

"But how—?"

"No phone in the house," T.J. said. "But the house is wired. I figured we needed help sooner rather than later, so I tripped the security alarm. It's silent. No one to hear it out here anyway."

"You tripped the alarm," she repeated. "But not until after you'd checked the house out."

He lifted his good shoulder in a half shrug. "An occupational skill. Never know when stuff like that will come in handy."

She stared at him.

T.J. could feel time slip away like a tangible thing. He grew serious. He had to make sure she didn't slip away from him. "I know this is all coming at you from left field, but I wanted to tell you up front what kind of man you'd be dealing with."

"I know what kind of man I'm dealing with," she

said. "Your occupation or lack of it makes no difference."

"I don't want to lose you, Jenna. Not when I just
found you. I have to go back to Denver and take care
of all of this. Then I want to come back here. I'm not
sure what I want to do, but I'm in good shape money-
wise. I'll have time to figure that out. I do know who
I'd like to spend time figuring it out with."

Her confusion cleared, and she held his gaze sol-
emnly, with what almost looked like . . . regret in
her eyes. "I don't know if I'll be here," she said.

T.J. felt as if someone had punched him in the
heart. The siren wail grew steadily louder. "Jenna,
I—"

"There are things you don't know about me either," she said seriously.

"Nothing that would stop me from wanting to see
you again." *From wanting to spend the rest of my life
with you.*

"Earlier, when I commented on the fires here, you
didn't ask me any questions. Why?"

"I didn't think you wanted to go through any
more at that moment. I figured you'd tell me in
time."

"Well, it doesn't look like I'll have that luxury
now."

T.J.'s eyes narrowed, but she didn't seem angry.
Her tone was even, resigned almost, rather than an-
gry. "I wanted more time too, but we need help,
Jenna. I—"

"I know, I know. I understand." She paused, then

said, "You remember I told you I had a partner named Toby."

He nodded, his muscles tightening in painful anxiety as the sirens drew closer. He wished now he'd gone to get her before alerting the damn security people.

"I am—was—a smoke jumper for the Forest Service. I fought forest fires."

T.J. had spent some time wondering what had put her in Paradise Canyon, but he hadn't come close to guessing correctly. One look in her eyes told him the whole story. "Jonny," he said quietly.

She nodded, knowing he understood. "Toby died trying to save me in a monster gobbler early last summer. A tree fell on my ankle, shattered it. But that was no excuse for what happened. I couldn't get my gear out in time. He shouldn't have—" She stopped abruptly and shook her head. "I'm not going to go into all of that here." She looked at him squarely. "The bottom line is I won't be going back to work either."

"I don't know much about smoke jumpers. I didn't think any of them were women."

"Not many. A few."

"Pretty tough job requirements, I'll bet."

"I held my own."

T.J. considered that along with the slight tilt to her chin. He smiled and dropped a quick kiss on it, right beneath her lips. "I bet you gave them hell."

"I'd say we broke about even." A ghost of a smile flickered around her mouth, but she remained serious. "During the off-season I worked for the Bureau of Land Management and at the jumper training school in Missoula."

T.J. regarded her for a moment. "You don't want to be a teacher either, do you?" It wasn't a question. "Have you thought about being a pilot? Jump planes or helicopters?"

She shook her head. "That's not something I've ever been interested in. And even if I wanted to teach, I couldn't. Instructors need to be in as good a shape as the trainees. I'll never be able to jump on this ankle again."

In that quietly spoken sentence, T.J. heard her real regret. He held her tighter, pressed her face to his chest, and nuzzled her neck. "You did this for Jonny, but you really loved it, didn't you, Jenna?"

She nodded silently. They remained that way for several seconds. The sirens were loud enough now that it was clear their time was up.

T.J. drew back and tilted her head up. "Will you go back to Paradise to work on your ankle again?"

She shook her head. "Will you for your knee?"

He shook his head. "I'll take care of that while I'm in Denver this time. Since I'm not going back to the Dozen, I won't push the rehab quite so hard this time."

"The Dozen?"

"My team. Long story." He couldn't will a grin to his face. Instead he pulled her tightly against him, not caring if he was tearing every remaining ligament in his shoulder. "I want to tell it to you, Jenna. I want to share everything with you. I don't want it to end here."

"Me either," she said, the words muffled against his chest.

His mouth sought hers at the same moment as she lifted her face to his. He took her hard and fast into the kiss, trying to communicate to her everything he had no time left to say. She responded with equal fervor, not lifting her mouth from his until the red flashing lights washed over them as two security cruisers swerved to a stop several feet away.

"I won't lose you, Jenna," he vowed against her lips. He pulled back and looked into her eyes, holding her gaze steadily even as the sound of car doors slamming and questioning voices intruded. "Don't lose me, either."

She wasn't given the chance to answer him. His only assurance as they separated was the promise he swore he saw in her eyes.

T.J. paced Scottie Giardi's Denver office, not even pausing to notice the magnificent view of the snowcapped Rockies the huge picture windows afforded. Actually, paced was a relative term. With the knee brace he had on, hobbled was probably more accurate.

The tall woman behind the desk regarded him steadily. "Will you please sit down? It hurts me to watch you."

T.J. ignored her request. Again. "How hard can it be to track down one woman?"

"We're trying, Delahaye."

"They own a huge ranch, for crying out loud."

"Which they put up for sale two weeks ago. Right before they packed up and left town."

"Hasn't anyone been able to locate them yet?"

"The report should come in sometime today."

T.J. swore under his breath; the frustration that had built up for the last month had reached critical mass.

The last he'd seen of Jenna had been from the rear window of the security cruiser as he'd been taken to the closest hospital some sixty miles away. She'd stayed behind.

After they explained the situation to the men who'd responded to the alarm, it had been quickly decided that T.J. required medical treatment well beyond the capabilities of Paradise Canyon. Jenna had argued against going to both the hospital and Paradise, but in the end had agreed to return to Paradise. And that had come only after she'd thoroughly satisfied herself that Bob would be taken care of.

She agreed to fill Paradise in on what had happened and to get X rays of her ankle and have her hands attended to. He'd managed to extract a promise that she'd go to the hospital if the Paradise staff recommended it. He'd also asked that if a hospital stay wasn't necessary, she wait long enough for him to contact her. She'd agreed.

As it turned out, he hadn't been able to make that

call until the following morning. He'd made it through a hellish night of examinations and probing and eventually rushed surgery, and through it all he'd focused on one thing: hearing her smoky voice on the telephone as soon as it was over. Telling her he loved her. Still groggy from the sedatives, he'd demanded a phone. He reached Paradise, but not Jenna.

He'd quickly abandoned his usual genial attitude, demanding that the tired technician repeat her statement twice before he let himself believe what he was hearing. She informed him that Ms. King's ankle had been severely sprained but that there had been no serious damage to the earlier surgical repairs. Her hands had been cleaned up and bandaged. She'd checked out shortly afterward. The only information he'd been able to obtain was that she'd returned a phone call from her parents, made earlier to her at Paradise, before leaving. No address, no nothing.

His behavior over the next week at the hospital hadn't won him any friends, but it had gotten him released early and put on a plane to Denver. He'd contacted Scottie from Oregon and asked her to help him track Jenna down. Scottie had wisely kept her questions to a minimum. They managed to get her address in Missoula, but she hadn't been back there. They contacted a few people who had worked with her, but all of them assumed she was still in Oregon. That left her parents. T.J. figured it was her call to them that had spurred her to leave Paradise so abruptly without letting someone know where she was going.

He had to believe that. The alternative was simply not acceptable. He refused to believe he'd misinterpreted what he'd seen in her eyes that night. Something had to have happened.

"But what the hell is it!" he demanded.

Scottie had been steadily taking calls, speaking in hushed tones as T.J. prowled the carpet like a wounded animal. She ignored his outburst as she gently replaced the receiver from her latest call and pushed to a stand. Coming around the desk, she didn't stop until she was right in front of him, forcing him to stop or plow her down.

She simply looked at him. T.J. thought again how she was the only woman he'd ever met who could look up at him and down her nose at the same time. Nothing ever fazed her. He'd seen her take on a crew of angry men and calm them without so much as raising her voice.

When Seve Delgado, the Dirty Dozen's original team leader, had been forced to leave and adopt a new life after testifying in a drug trial, he'd handpicked Scottie to take over. No one on the team had disagreed with his choice. In fact, most of them had been relieved.

She agreed only to a temporary assignment until a new leader could be chosen. But the team had suffered heavy losses over the years, some due to fatalities, others to casualties of the heart. Scottie had looked at these unforeseen developments and seen new possibilities. She'd taken the team in an entirely new direction, creating a home-based task force whose function was to coordinate things from Denver, where they would also train replacements so the team wouldn't find itself in its current situation ever again. She'd done such an outstanding job that, after much pleading and downright harassment from the remaining team members, she'd recently agreed to take the job as leader permanently.

But Scottie hadn't been resting on her laurels. She'd heard T.J.'s announcement of his retirement and all of his carefully thought-out reasons for his decision with calm equanimity. And she'd spent every second since trying to convince him to come and work on the inside with the other "new hearts," as she termed the two recent members of the team who had dropped out of fieldwork to marry. In fact, she'd gotten the wives involved also. She was a hard woman to turn down. T.J. thought he'd held up admirably.

Looking at Scottie now, he thought his luck might have run out.

"Sit down." She didn't wait for him to answer but moved toward a small grouping of sectional couches arranged around a large square coffee table in the corner of her office. She sat and crossed her long, jean-clad legs. Scottie may have "come in from the cold," but she had her own ideas about what constituted "power dressing" and she'd held fast to them despite the gold lettering on her office door.

Knowing he'd get nowhere until he did as she asked, T.J. followed, and after some serious negotiating with the coffee table and the hinges on his knee brace, finally settled across from his former boss.

"Can I ask you something, T.J.?"

Scottie rarely called him T.J. It was the only thing that kept him from exploding in frustration. "Ask," he said tightly.

"When I took this job, Del mentioned something to me that at the time I didn't think about much. He was talking about his reunion with his daughter and said something about finding Diego in here pacing like a wounded bear. Since I took over for Del, I've come in here to find two more of you pacing this office in a similar condition. Come to think of it, you were all wounded literally as well. What is it with you guys? A woman has to beat you up to get your attention?"

She surprised a smile out of him. "Personal questions, Giardi?" By necessity, the Dirty Dozen crew were all notoriously private. Scottie had long been acknowledged as the Queen of the Loners.

"Curiosity. Is Jenna the reason you won't come to work for me here?"

"No. I explained all—"

She waved a hand with uncharacteristic impatience. "I know what you told me. I'm not asking about what's up here." She tapped her forehead. "I'm talking about what's in here." She covered her heart with her hand.

T.J. shook his head. "I'd already come to this decision before meeting her. Being back in Oregon . . ." He trailed off, suddenly unable to find the words. He looked out the window, then back to her. "It's home. I didn't expect to feel that. Never thought of myself as really having a home. He gestured toward the window and the sprawl of buildings stretched out below that was Denver. "I've lived here longer than anywhere and, hell, I was hardly ever here." He paused for a moment, then said, "I never missed it when I was gone. I never even thought about it. Denver is just a base to touch before hitting the road again. It wasn't until I got to Oregon that I realized I'd never let myself miss anything."

"How did you know?"

"Because I was glad to be back," he answered, the truth of it coming easily now. "But mostly because I didn't want to leave."

"Leave Jenna, you mean."

He shook his head. "No, this part has nothing to do with Jenna. I mean leave home. I didn't want to leave home." He leaned forward. "Scottie, I'm done here. I want to go home."

She nodded in acceptance, but he could see she didn't truly understand. Hell, a few months ago, he wouldn't have either.

"What are you going to do?" she asked.

He shrugged. "Not sure yet."

She raised her eyebrows a fraction. "Good plan."

T.J. grinned. "Hey, you know they keep us too busy to spend any of the pile of money they pay us. I have time."

"You don't sound too worried about it."

He'd been too worried about Jenna to think about it, but now that she'd said it, he realized she was right. "No, I'm not. I'm on the right path. I'll find my way."

A part of his soul felt as if it had been set free. The other part was still locked away. Only one woman had the key.

"You don't know what you want," she said. "But you do know who."

"I'm in no hurry to get to the end of this new path, Scottie. But yes, I do know who I want to explore it with."

"A woman you knew for less than twenty-four hours and who walked away from you without so much as a good-bye or forwarding address?"

She hadn't spoken harshly, and T.J. didn't take it that way. In fact, she seemed to be genuinely interested in his answer.

"Yes. Not a doubt in my mind."

Scottie's shrug seemed to say she'd given up on ever understanding it. "What if her 'path' isn't yours?"

"That's for her to decide. I'm betting it's the same."

Scottie made a disgusted noise. "Men. If I had a million years, I'd never figure you guys out."

He grinned. "Funny, we've been saying the same thing about you."

That did elicit a smile from her.

T.J.'s smile faded. "Thank you, Scottie," he said quietly.

"For what?" She looked honestly surprised.

"For taking the time to help me with this. I quit on you, and I know it's a bad time what with all the changes and—"

"T.J., that's what friends do."

That shut him up. He sat there for a long moment, for the first time realizing that he might not miss Denver, but he would miss his team. "We work so hard at maintaining our rigid invulnerability," he said quietly. "We're all loners; no ties, no families. And yet there isn't a person on this team who wouldn't risk his life to save a teammate, and not just for the sake of the mission. We've become our own odd sort of family in spite of ourselves. I guess no one is truly alone."

Something bleak flashed in her eyes, but it was gone too fast for him to pin down. "Well, Delahaye, we are still human."

He was back to being Delahaye. The phone beeped, cutting off any comment he might have made. Scottie got up and crossed quickly to answer it. T.J. felt the tension return tenfold. By the time he'd managed to stand, she was done. "Well?"

"I think we've got something," she said in her crisp no-nonsense contralto. "Do you know someone named Bob?"

Jenna heard a car in the drive. "Finally," she said, and hurried to the front door of her parents' ranch house to let the real-estate agent in. The woman had been due over an hour earlier. She was bringing a "Sold" sign and some papers for Jenna to sign. Only when Jenna swung open the door, it wasn't the real-estate lady's gleaming white Grand Cherokee she found in the driveway. Instead she found a dark blue one-ton pickup with a matching horse trailer attached to the back.

She stepped out onto the porch, limping slightly on her almost-healed ankle, intending to tell the gentleman opening the driver's-side door that the last of the stock had been sold a week before.

But the man who unfolded himself from the oversized cab wasn't a local rancher come to take advantage of a neighbor's sudden decision to sell everything lock, stock, and barrel and move to Arizona. In fact, the man wasn't a rancher at all.

Jenna shielded her eyes against the bright winter sun, shivering beneath her sweater and jeans. "T.J.?" It came out as a whisper and sounded more like a prayer.

He was wearing a sheep-lined jacket over worn blue jeans and Western boots. The battered Stetson he retrieved from the seat and plopped on his head completed the outfit. It looked so natural on him, she'd have sworn he'd been born on a horse. Even the ugly concoction of metal frames and padding strapped around his knee didn't detract from the overall aura that he exuded. The aura of pure, unadulterated man. Her man.

The very idea had her faltering at the top step.

He made his way to the bottom of the wide porch stairs, moving fairly easily. He doffed his hat as he looked up at her.

Her heart was pounding in her chest like a locomotive. She'd never wanted anything as badly as she

wanted T. J. Delahaye. But a frustrating and ulti-
mately fruitless month spent searching for him, expecting him to show up any second, while also dealing
with the sudden upheaval in her family had her coming to terms with several harsh realities. The harshest
being that he was never coming back. She'd lost him
for good.

"I was expecting the real-estate agent," she said,
proud of her flat tone.

"I met her at the end of the drive," he said.

His voice was deeper and richer than she'd remembered. She locked her knees and resisted the
urge to smooth her hair.

"She gave me some papers for you to sign.
They're in the truck."

"I'm not sure I can say good-bye to you twice,"
she said in response, already feeling her control slipping. "So why don't you tell me why you're here so
we can get this over with."

"And here I'd worried that you'd pine away and
go soft on me." He took a step closer. "Hello, Jenna.
Can I come in?"

She narrowed her gaze, not willing to let hope
take even a toehold on her heart. Yet. "Will it take
that long?"

She thought she saw pain and vulnerability flash
across his face but decided it was probably the sun
playing tricks on her. In their brief time together,
he'd taught her so much. But the lesson she clung to
now was the last one. Hope was painful.

"It's taken me a month to find you," he said. "Can you at least give me a few minutes?"

He'd spent a month tracking her down? "I've been here the whole time." Except for the exhausting three-day vigil she'd held at the hospital waiting to see if her father would live or die. "You could have gotten the address and phone number from Paradise." She'd gotten the message from her mother within minutes of her arrival that night. She'd left a message with the hospital for her mother to call back and then kept her word and gotten her ankle and hands looked after.

"I called you the next morning," he said. "I had emergency surgery. All they told me was that you were gone and you hadn't said where you were going."

"But they knew I'd talked to my mother, they knew about my dad. They—"

"They told me that. I'm sorry about your dad, Jenna. Is he doing okay?"

She nodded numbly. "He and Mom are already in Arizona. He has emphysema and severe arthritis. His doctors have been recommending the move for years." But it took almost dying in the arms of his wife and daughter to make him do it. The long hours spent waiting with her mother had given them both time to talk . . . and heal. For the first time they'd talked about Jonny. There had been tears and recriminations, along with hugs and vows of continuing communication. Nothing would be solved easily, but they'd made a beginning.

"I agreed to sell the ranch for them so they could leave right away before Dad changed his mind. Stubborn fool." She thought she caught T.J. stifling a smile, but he didn't say anything.

Then his expression grew serious. "It must have been hard coming back here."

His insight didn't surprise her, but the warm feeling of security she felt did. Oh, what it was like to have someone to share with. Someone who truly understood. "At first. I left soon after Jonny died and have only been back a few times. I thought I hated ranching, hated everything about this place. But instead of loathing it, I found out that I'd really missed it. All of it."

"Did you talk to your folks about it?" he asked quietly.

She stilled. All she could do was nod. She'd spent the last two weeks awash in feelings and emotions and not a few regrets. She was only beginning to sort through them all. But one thing she'd understood all along was how she felt about this man. That she hadn't had the guts to keep fighting until she found him, the way he apparently had, shamed her. She thought she'd stopped playing victim. He'd been the one to teach her to trust again. She'd let them both down.

"I'm sorry about the confusion, T.J.," she said finally, all defensiveness gone. *More than you'll ever know.* "I assumed they had my parents' information and would give it to you. I . . . I looked for you too." *And assumed too easily you didn't want to be found.* Heat filled her cheeks.

"I've had half my team out trying to hunt you down," he said. "I've been to Missoula, I've—"

"You went to Missoula?"

"I knew that was where you were from. I spoke to your team commander."

"You talked to Bucky?"

"Yep. He's the one who put me in touch with Mrs. Ventura."

"Mrs. Ventura, but she's—" Jenna's hand flew up to cover her mouth.

"Toby's mother," he finished. There was a pause, then he said, "I know how hard it must have been to talk to her. I'm proud of you, Jenna."

"I spent a long time talking with my mom at the hospital. I . . . I realized that was only the beginning, that to heal fully I had to face all of my demons." And yet she'd given up on the man who'd taught her how to heal in the first place. She'd never felt less proud of herself. She loved this man, yet she'd given up, hadn't trusted in him, or herself.

"I know it helped Mrs. Ventura a great deal."

She wanted to clap her hands over her ears. I'm a fraud, she wanted to tell him. Couldn't he see she didn't deserve this? He should be angry, not proud.

T.J. studied her, and for a moment she thought he might say something. She realized she wanted him to, wanted him to once again show her how to heal when it was her own damn responsibility. She added cowardice to her list of sins.

"Why did you come back?"

In a sudden move, T.J. grabbed the railing and hopped the steps so swiftly, Jenna didn't even have time to back up. He lifted his hands, to hug her or shake her she didn't know, but he dropped them without touching her. "Because I want to go home. And I can't go without you."

THIRTEEN

Black velvet, that's what his voice was. Soft and smooth, his words rippled over her, gathering her scattered thoughts, giving them a chance to fall back into an understandable pattern. And she did understand. He didn't deserve better than her, he just deserved a better her.

"I gave up on you, T.J." She looked up into his eyes, a part of her marveling over the rush it gave her that she had to look up at all. "I shouldn't have," she said quietly. "Once I knew my dad was going to be okay, I called the hospital in Oregon, but you were gone. You weren't at Paradise, and you're not listed anywhere in Denver." She held his gaze. "I did try, T.J." She shivered and rubbed her arms as a cold breeze swept the porch. "But not hard enough. When you didn't find me, I started thinking you didn't want me." Her heart broke and melted at the same time at the stab of pain she saw in his eyes. "It was easier to believe that than it was to trust my heart, face my fears, and risk finding the truth. I thought I was healing myself by moving on, but I was hiding again. You taught me better than that, T.J. I'm sorry. So sorry."

He framed her face with his hands. The healing force of his touch exceeded her memories. "Jenna, you've faced more in the last month than most people do in a lifetime. The only thing you're guilty of is being too hard on yourself." He crowded her back against the front door, blocking the winter wind. "You're cold. Can we go inside now?"

She could only nod but didn't move for the handle. He didn't move either. Instead they both gazed steadily into each other's eyes.

"I thought I'd lost you," he said roughly.

"For a while I thought I'd lost everything," she said.

He frowned. For the first time she saw something that looked very much like fear in his eyes. That she could scare him scared her too.

"Do you still want to find me, Jenna?"

"More than ever."

"Thank God," he breathed, pulling her tightly into his arms. He buried his face in her hair as she snaked her arms around his waist.

She held him as tightly as she could, thrilling at the realization that she didn't have to moderate her strength, thrilling even further when he moaned, "Tighter, Jenna. You can't be too close."

He finally tilted her head up and looked into her eyes. There were still questions there, lots of them.

But Jenna knew they'd have time to answer them all. The fear was gone.

"Take me inside, Jenna."

His request raised dark erotic images that she wasn't entirely certain he'd meant, but she intended to do her damnedest to find out.

She smiled at him. "We'd better. If I start kissing you out here, we'll both freeze to death."

"There's one thing I have to do first." He reached behind her and caught the end of her braid. She watched as he removed the braided elastic. He slowly unwound the heavy plait like a man unwrapping a precious gift. He spread the thick waves around her shoulders. "I've waited a lifetime to do that," he said roughly. He sank his fingers into the wavy mass and cupped the back of her head.

A hot thrill shot through her as she read the intent clear in his blue eyes.

His mouth was on hers before she got the door all the way open. He didn't stop once they were inside and backwalked her straight down the hall until the closet door stopped their progress. Jenna kept his mouth firmly on hers as she shifted and backed into her bedroom, not stopping until she felt the bed at the back of her knees.

Only when the sweet weight of T.J.'s big body was spread out over every glorious inch of hers did he lift his head. "I love you, Jenna. I won't lose you ever again."

"I love you too, T.J." She yanked his head down for a hard fast kiss. Then pushed him away just enough to look into his eyes. "And you bet your sweet backside you won't." She pinched the aforementioned body part, which made him grind his hips down on hers, eliciting a long moan. "Just how hard is it to get that knee brace off anyway?"

T.J. chuckled and stole a heart-stopping kiss of his own. "What did I do to deserve such a gorgeous, smartmouthed, stubborn woman like you?"

She looked up at him, and her heart swelled almost to bursting with the love she found there. She vowed then and there to be the woman he deserved. The knowledge that he'd never let her be less fueled the sassy smile that curved her lips. "Who else would have you?"

"We'll never know. I'm yours, and it's a lifetime deal. Take it or leave it."

"Oh, I take it." She looked up at him, eyes sparkling. "Question is, can you?"

T.J. bent his head to capture her smart mouth, but she pushed him back just shy of his quarry. "One question first."

Second-guessing her, he said, "I quit my job. I want to buy some land in Oregon, but we can decide on that later. I'll support any direction you want to go with your career, and I have a pile of money saved up so we don't have to worry about that for at least the next few hours and—"

She pressed her fingers to his lips. "I know we'll work that out." Her tone was serious, but her eyes were shining with the bright promise that was their future.

His need for her didn't lessen one iota, but suddenly it wasn't as urgent to assuage all those needs in the next two seconds. She really wasn't going anywhere. She was truly and completely his. "Do I really get to marry you and spend the rest of my life with you?" he whispered.

"You're stuck with me all right."

"Then ask me anything. What do you want to know, my love?"

"What's in the trailer?"

"The trail—?" T.J.'s answer was interrupted by a sudden ruckus erupting beyond the bedroom window in the front yard. Loud banging and thumping followed by a high-pitched wail.

Jenna grabbed his head and turned his face back to hers. "Tell me you didn't."

She looked dead serious. He didn't pretend to misunderstand. In fact, he'd been looking forward to this moment. He enthusiastically anticipated a lifetime full of them. "I want a family," he began slowly. The noise outside got worse. She grew more rigid beneath him but he pressed on. Her eyes narrowed so he hurried on. "But we never talked about things like babies and all that—"

"I like babies."

That stopped him cold. "You do?"

"Mmm-hmm."

She was smiling that serene smile and a new thought suddenly occurred to him. His heart stopped. "You're not . . . I mean, I would love it if you were, don't get me wrong. But that's not why you were looking for me. Was it?"

She laughed and shook her head. "No, I'm not. And I was looking for you because I love you. More with each passing second." She squeezed him tightly. "Tell me more about this family plan of yours. I'm dying to hear," she said dryly.

She was still smiling, but now that the idea had occurred to him, it took him a second or two to get past the image of her lying in his arms, her stomach round with their child. . . . He sighed as he kissed her, then said, "I'm thinking of modifying the plan," he said. "Soon."

"I like that plan. But first I want to know more about the family member you already adopted."

Defeated by her intractability, he switched tactics. "Jenna, I couldn't let strangers raise him."

"I found him a very good home, T.J. Mrs. Ventura was right when she said the Peebleses ran a very respectable ranch."

"But, honey—"

"Most families buy a dog or a cat if they want a pet."

"But you love Bob."

"He spit on me, T.J. Dogs and cats don't spit."

Her tone hadn't changed, but T.J. didn't let that stop him. He nuzzled her neck, hoping to distract her from the sounds of Bob bashing at the new trailer he'd bought just for him. Well, not just for him . . . He licked a small trail from her ear to her collarbone and, based on her instant reaction, decided it was quite effective, so he upped the ante and slid his hands under her sweater.

"I'll feed him and take care of him," he promised. "I'll buy you a dog if you want."

"I don't want a dog."

He lifted his head, willing to beg even though he was enjoying their discussion immensely.

She immediately dragged it back down. "Don't stop," she ordered. "I'm weakening."

"Not on your worst day," he said, but quickly followed up with another foray, heading down her belly.

She gasped when he slid her zipper down. "Okay, okay, we'll keep Bob. But only if you promise not to stop."

"I promise," he said, his words muffled against the sweet skin of her thigh. "I like arguing with you." He thought about telling her the rest, then figured he'd wait until he was inside her to mention the other one. But that seemed cowardly. He wasn't going to start this relationship backing down from Jenna. She'd never forgive him.

He lifted his head, despite the iron grip she had on the back of it. "Llamas hate being alone."

"So will you if you don't keep your promise."

He chuckled and blew gently across her skin.

"T.J." But there was nothing demanding in her tone this time. She sounded . . . needy. He liked that side of her too.

Between kisses and nibbles he said, "Bob has a . . . friend."

Jenna reached down and grabbed his shoulders,

hauling him—with his willing if awkward assistance—
back up on top of her until they were face-to-face.
"There are two of them out there?"

"Don't worry, they can't hurt each other."

"Two llamas?"

He nodded but didn't say anything.

She pulled him down for a long, deep, wet kiss,
instead. "You know what?" she asked when she let
him up for air. "We can have a whole ranch of them if
that's what you want."

He cocked his head to one side. "Well, now that
you mention it—"

Laughing even as she groaned, she said, "I'm mar-
rying a rancher. A llama rancher at that. My dad will
never let me hear the end of it."

"Jenna, if you don't—"

"I do," she quickly assured him. "In fact, since
you mentioned buying land in Oregon . . . I was
thinking maybe we'd check and see if Bob's ranch is
still on the market."

T.J. went still, then grew serious. "Jenna, are you
sure? I mean, there are plenty of—"

"T.J.," she said, gently interrupting him. "I'm
sure. In fact, I think it's perfect. It's what I need. A
chance to rebuild on the ruins of the past."

T.J. saw the rightness of it in her eyes. "You'll
want the stalls done first." At the question in her eyes,
he said, "For the horses."

She hugged him close. "Make love to me, T.J."
With a wicked smile, she added, "Who knows, maybe

we can add another Martha or George to carry on the Delahaye name."

He grinned and framed her face with his hands. "I love you, Jenna."

"I love you too, Thomas Jefferson Delahaye."

Sometime later, when night had fallen and the llamas were tucked away in their stalls, she lay curled against T.J.'s chest. "You know, it might take a while for me to get pregnant."

T.J. just laughed. Jenna smacked his chest, but giggled too. "Seriously, I think we ought to change Bob's name to Abraham or Ulysses. Of course, there is the female to consider. I know! JFK and Jackie O. Someday we'll have a little Caroline or John John llama."

He lifted his head. "His name is Bob," he stated flatly. "I was thinking of calling the female Babe."

She groaned. "The Paul Bunyan thing again? But that was just a joke, T.J. I mean, really. I think—"

He pulled her under him. "Think about this instead."

For once she didn't argue. T.J. smiled. She sure picked her moments.

THE EDITORS' CORNER

It's hard to believe that autumn is here! Soon Old Man Winter will be making his way down our paths, and we'll all be complaining about the cold weather instead of the oppressive heat. One thing you won't be complaining about is the Loveswept November lineup. And trust us, Old Man Winter doesn't stand a chance with these sexy men on the prowl!

Timing is everything, so they say, and Suzanne Brockmann proves the old adage true with her next LOVESWEPT, #858, **TIME ENOUGH FOR LOVE**. Chuck Della Croce has a problem. His time machine is responsible for a tragedy that has resulted in the deaths of hundreds. Thinking he can go back in time to literally save the world, Chuck ends up on Maggie Winthrop's doorstep. Maggie can't help but notice the stranger who's obnoxiously banging on her door, especially since he's naked as a jaybird! When he tells her he's from the future, she's ready to call the men in white coats, but something about him gives her pause. As Chuck explains his mission to prevent a disaster and save her life, Maggie must learn to accept that anything is possible. Suzanne Brockmann guides us in a timeless journey and persuades us to believe in the powers of destiny and second chances.

Eyes meeting across a crowded room, sexual tension building to a crescendo . . . *bam!*, you've got yourself a Loveswept! That certainly is the recipe conjured up in LOVESWEPT #859, **RELATIVE STRANGERS**, by Kathy Lynn Emerson. A ghost is lurking in the halls of Sinclair House, one who is anxious to reunite with her own true love. But first she must bring together the hearts of Lucas Sinclair and Corrie Ballantyne. Unfortunately, the two won't cooperate. Strange occurrences involving Corrie keep happening at Lucas's historic hotel, and he needs to get to the bottom of things before the place goes under. After seeing the ghosts of Lucas's ancestors, Corrie must decide if it's her own desire that draws her to him, or if it's the will of another. Can Corrie make peace with the past by unearthing hidden truths and soothing the unspoken sorrows of the man she will love forever? Kathy Lynn Emerson's exquisitely romantic ghost story is downright irresistible in both its sensuality and its mystery.

Trapped on an island with a hurricane on the loose, Trevor Fox and Jana Jenkins seek **SHELTER FROM THE STORM**, LOVESWEPT #860 by Maris Soule. Cursing a storm that had grounded all his charters, Trevor was only too glad to agree to lend a hand to the alluring seductress with the pouty lips.

Little did he know that his day would go from bad to worse, and from there to . . . well, whatever comes after that. Held at gunpoint, he is forced to fly to the Bahamas, and into the path of a hurricane. Jana Jenkins just wants to live a quiet, uneventful life, but when her stepbrother is kidnapped, Jana does what's necessary to save him—even if that includes dragging this brash pirate with a tarnished reputation along for the ride. Loveswept veteran Maris Soule knows there's nothing like a little danger to spice up the lives of a woman on the run and a man who enjoys the chase!

Dr. Kayla Davies learns just what will be her **UL-TIMATE SURRENDER**, LOVESWEPT #861 by Jill Shalvis, an author who is penning her way into our hearts. When Kayla and her ex–brother-in-law, Ryan Scott, are summoned to the home of a beloved aunt, the two must make peace with their past and with each other. There's no love lost between the ruthless police detective and Kayla, but Ryan can't understand the fear he sees lurking in the depths of her blue eyes. As Kayla grows to know Ryan, she finds herself in the strange position of being both attracted and repelled by the man she once believed evil. Trapped in a web of old deceits, Ryan and Kayla struggle together to silence the ghosts of their past. But if Kayla dares to confess her dark secret, can Ryan find the strength to forgive? Writing with touching emotion and tender sensuality, Jill Shalvis once again proves that love can be a sweet victory over heart-break.

Happy reading!

With warmest regards,

Susann Brailey *Joy Abella*

Susann Brailey Joy Abella

Senior Editor Administrative Editor